GHOST DANCE

By Susan Price
PUBLISHED BY FARRAR, STRAUS AND GIROUX

Ghost Dance
Ghost Song
The Ghost Drum ·

GHOST DANCE

The Czar's Black Angel

SUSAN PRICE

Farrar, Straus and Giroux
New York

Copyright © 1994 by Susan Price
All rights reserved
First published in Great Britain by Faber and Faber Ltd., 1994
Printed in the United States of America
First American Edition, 1995

Library of Congress Cataloging-in-Publication Data
Price, Susan.
Ghost dance : the czar's black angel / Susan Price.
—1st American ed.
p.   cm.
[1. Fantasy.   2. Lapps—Fiction.   3. Russia—Fiction.]   I. Title
PZ7.P9317Gf   1994   [Fic]—dc20   94-9841   CIP   AC

GHOST DANCE

1

In a place far distant from where you are now grows an oak tree by a lake.

Round the oak's trunk is a chain of golden links.

Tethered to the chain is a learned cat, and this most learned of all cats walks round and round the tree continually.

As it walks one way, it sings songs.

As it walks the other, it tells stories.

This is one of the stories the cat tells.

I tell (says the cat) of the Northlands, where, in the long, dark winter, the white snow falls out of the black, black sky. Soft, silent it falls through the branches of the pines and birch, and mounts, thin flake on thin flake, until the snow lies ten cold feet deep, and the silence is frozen to the darkness.

This (says the cat) is the land where that white, sharp-backed horse, North Wind, carries Granddad Frost swiftly through the trees. The old man breathes to the left and right, and what his breath touches is blasted and withered, and his rasping voice whispers, 'Are you cold, children? Are you cold?'

I tell (says the cat) of a gyrfalcon flying – a bird the colour of snow in darkness, flying above snow and through darkness. It turned in sweeping circles, it gyred, and its sickle-winged shadow scudded before it over the moonlit snow far beneath.

The gyrfalcon looked down and saw a flat circle of the Earth tipped up to its gaze. A circle of Earth gleaming white, but marked with black rocks, with black trees, and all growing smaller as the falcon gyred upwards; all growing greater as it spun down. The only sounds the falcon hears are the soft huff of wind under its wings, and its own cry, thin and sharp as wire drawn from ice: *Keeee-ya! Keeee-ya!*

A gyrfalcon's eyes can outstare the sun, and now they pierced the winter darkness. It saw a tree, and its eyes stared, and saw the cones in its branches; and stared, and saw each needle leaf. And stared, and saw the mice running up the trunk.

Its eyes stared down, and saw the rocks; and stared and saw the cracks in the rocks; and stared and saw the voles that hid there. It stared down and saw the fox making tracks across the snow. It saw the fish beneath the ice.

It wheeled in the sky and looked down and saw the tents of the reindeer people, and the reindeer, and the wolves following, and the ever-hungry glutton hurrying among the trees. It saw the snow-rabbit and the lynx and the bear.

But of all these things, trees and people, deer and wolves, fish and lynx, fox and bear, the gyrfalcon saw fewer, far fewer than before. And it saw bloodied places in the snow, and twisted, frozen bodies in traps; and the cut stumps of trees. *Keeee-ya! Keeee-ya!*

Then the gyrfalcon's eyes sharpened on what it searched for, and it wheeled in the cold sky and circled down. Below, a small line of men, black against the snow, slid on skis through the pines. Lower the falcon gyred, and lower, staring on the men.

I'll tell of the men (says the cat). They were hunters, and hungry. The snow was so deep that they were raised high among the tree branches and skimmed through them like birds. All of them looked like fat old men, with their round bodies and their white beards – but their fatness was the thick, warm padding of their clothes; and their beards were not white with age, but with ice frozen to the hair. All of them skied with their heads ducked low, to keep their faces from the scraping of the wind-blown ice, and they gripped bows in their mittened hands, and wore hoods or tall caps with flaps to cover their ears. Quivers of arrows rustled and thumped at their sides, but no game. They had caught nothing.

They peered from side to side as they went, for the wind carried a load of ice-crystals that rattled and crackled in the cold air, and made a shifting white, grey, ice-blue veil before their eyes. The wind would drop, and let the ice fall, crackling, to the snow, and the black trees would stand out clear against the white, the silver stars bright against the black. But then the wind would lift up the ice and snow once more, and the stars dimmed, and the trees would seem to shrink or grow, or even to leave the Earth and walk, when seen through that shifting, icy cloud.

A whiteness swooped at the men and they skidded to

a halt, snow spurting from their skis. They ducked and cried out as the gyrfalcon came swinging towards them again. With upraised wings, it dropped from the sky into the snow, and turned into – what? Too small for a man. A boy?

The figure straightened from a crouch and stood before them, its booted feet denting the frozen surface of the snow. The hunters reached to their quivers for arrows, and fitted them to their bowstrings.

A lad – or a girl. A girl, or a lad, who had dropped out of a tree – or out of the sky. A lad, or a girl, alone, so far from any camp or settlement – and dressed, in this cold and darkness, as if for a stroll on a summer evening. Boots, yes, hide boots like theirs, embroidered and patterned; but above the boots only a tunic and breeches of thin reindeer hide, stitched with brass rings, with tiny mirrors that flashed a dimmed white light, with bunches of tiny bones and bunches of white feathers. But no gloves and no hat – the stranger's long black hair blew about in the wind, and was quickly turning white with snow, as if this youngster were growing old in moments.

The hunters knew that no one living could endure such cold, dressed so lightly. They dared not take their eyes from the creature to look at each other, but all of them feared, in their own minds, that this was the ghost of one frozen to death, searching for others to soothe to freezing death in the snow.

The stranger came closer and, in the light reflected from the snow, they could see the face of one of their own people. But it could have been the face of a pretty

4

boy or a handsome girl. The stranger stretched out a naked hand and placed it on the arm of the hunters' leader.

'Are you cold, Uncle?' the stranger asked, just as Frost is said to ask. The voice was that of a boy, but croaking and quiet, as if the cold had withered it. 'I've been sent to find you.'

The hunters looked at each other, hoping one of them would know what to do. Some bent their bows further, ready to send an arrow into the ghost. Their leader, with the stranger's hand still on his wrist, looked into the boy-girl's face and asked, 'Who sent you to find us?'

'My grandmother.' The hoarse voice seemed surprised. 'Are you not searching for a shaman? I'm sent to bring you to her.'

The hunters gasped, sending puffs of their white breath into the darkness before their faces – breath which froze into icicles on their beards. They drew back from the stranger – all but the leader, who stood as if the hand on his wrist held him to the spot. Those with bent bows hastily let them down, took the arrows from the strings and put them back into their quivers as if no thought of shooting at the shaman's grandchild had been in their minds. It is never wise to offend a shaman. But they were not made happy by the stranger's words.

'Go with this forest ghost? Too dangerous!'

'We must! Haven't we proved a shaman can't be found by looking? Haven't we looked and looked and never found a trace of one?'

'It's an ice-devil! It will breathe in our faces and freeze us to death!'

5

The leader, still standing face to face with the stranger, said, 'How can we tell if we can trust you?'

In the hoarse voice that seemed always about to choke into silence, the young stranger said, 'If my grandmother meant to hurt you, Uncle, she could have done it without sending me within reach of your arrows. If I had meant to hurt you, I could have done it before you ever saw me.'

The leader nodded. 'Go on. I'll follow.' He slithered around on his skis and said to his friends, 'You can stay here, or go home, if you like.'

'I'll come!' said one.

'And I,' said another, shamefaced; and the rest grumbled that they would come too.

The young stranger gave a wide, white smile, turned and ran away over the snow. The frozen surface crunched and creaked beneath the running steps, but did not break; and the hunters pushed with their bows and slid swiftly after on their skis as the running figure vanished in the snow-mist and waveringly reappeared.

The runner leaped, spread arms that feathered and beat and lifted – and the white gyrfalcon was flying, sweeping high and circling and swooping down to flash white before their faces. *Keeee-ya!* It led them, a moon-white bird, through the black trees, over the white snow, under the black sky.

The hunters followed, skimming over the snow, the leaders intent on keeping the bird in sight. Those who came behind, with less to think of, were more nervous, and looked back into the cold and dark. The wind followed them, whispering, in the rattle and rustle of its shaken ice-crystals, 'Are you cold, my children? Are you cold?'

The falcon led them through the trees, through the snow-grey darkness and wind, to a snow-covered mound among the pines. But thin stripes of yellow light poked from the mound and fell across the snow, and they saw that it was a small house, with snow piled high on its roof and plastered to its sides, until it seemed a house built of snow planks, with snow carving, snow shutters and snow sills – a house roofed with snow shingles. Only the smoking stove-pipe poking from the roof was free of snow.

But, though the snow was so deep, the door of the house was above the frozen surface. The hunters sent frightened looks to each other. They feared that the house door was raised above the snow because, beneath the snow, hidden, were crouched a pair of giant chicken-legs. In all the stories they had ever heard, shamans lived in houses that walked on chicken-legs. And, indeed, as they slid nearer the house through the stinging grey mist, they heard a soft crooning, clucking noise, like that of a sleepy chicken.

The gyrfalcon wheeled around and about the little house, screaming its shrill, cold cry, and then dropped to the snow, and turned as it dropped into that pretty boy or handsome girl.

The hunters stopped, jostling into each other, those behind peering over the shoulders of those before. They had all heard, and told, stories of shamans, and to be there, in front of a shaman's hut, was frightening, like finding the gingerbread cottage.

'Come in from the cold,' said the shaman's grand-child.

The leader slid over to the house, and took off his skis. With hissings and scrapings of wooden runners over ice, the others joined him. They stuck the skis, and their bows, upright in the snow around the house, and they hung back, to let their leader be the first to follow the shaman's grandchild into the little house.

Once their leader had stepped through the outer door, the others crowded after, afraid to be left outside, and the small, dark space between the double doors was full of pushing and shoving until the inner door was opened and let them into the hut's single room.

It was a wooden room, a gold and cream and white room of split wood, and its air was hung with a thin, glimmering curtain of candlelight, all dusty with wood-scented dust. In the corners, shadows hung down from the ceiling like thick cobwebs. On the walls hung lutes, rattles, flutes and a big, oval drum, its skin painted with red signs which drew the stares of all the hunters. They knew it for a ghost drum, the very badge of a shaman. The light of the candles made white flares in the polish of the instruments, and deep shadows between them and the walls.

The stove had made the room so hot that the hunters sweated in their heavy clothes and tugged off their caps and mittens and opened the fronts of their coats. The shaman's grandchild knelt to help the leader off with his boots, and the other men leaned on each other as they kicked off their own boots. The shaman's grand-child collected all their coats and hats from them, throwing them into a heap on a chest against the wall.

In the centre of the room was a wooden table, set about with wooden benches and stools, and the table was crammed with dishes of black bread and jugs of vodka, bowls of dried fish and cheese and fruit. The hunters looked at it all, mouths watering, but too shy to ask if the food was for them. They had all been taught that a guest should be given a seat, food, drink and warmth before being asked a single question, but they had not expected a shaman to be so welcoming.

'Sit, Uncles, eat,' said the shaman's grandchild, and the hunters clambered over benches and hooked stools to them with their feet. Before their backsides were on the wood, their hands were reaching for the food and putting it into their mouths. They were hungry.

At the other end of the room was a small bed-closet, with wooden doors that could be closed against draughts. The doors were carved with interlacing lines, and hearts, and deer nibbling at trees whose branches were full of flowers and birds. One of the closet doors stood open, and the shaman's grandchild went over to this open door, and sat on the bed.

The hunters' leader looked up, his mouth full of bread and fish, and saw the other door of the bed-closet swing open. In the deep shadows within the bed sat someone small and hunched, peering out at them. A little, thin hand, twisted with knots of veins, reached out into the candlelight and took the hand of the youngster who sat on the end of the bed.

The hunters' leader raised his glass of vodka to the old woman in the bed, whom he could hardly see. 'To you, Grandmother! Thank you for this welcome! Long life and good luck to you!'

From within the bed's deep shadows came an old, cracked laugh. A scraping voice, almost worn away by age and use, said, 'The long life I have had, son; the luck I have made – but I thank you for your good wishes. Eat all you want – it's cold outside! And while you eat, tell me why you search for a shaman.'

'Here,' said the hunters' leader and, standing, he pulled free something that was tucked under his belt. He threw it to the youngster. 'Show your granny that. Can she say what kind of animal it came from?'

The thing was a small hide, oval in shape, and covered with a long, fine hair. The youngster turned it over and over, and stroked the long hair, puzzled.

The old voice from within the bed said, 'Put it on your head, little pancake, then you will see – it's the skin and hair from a man's head.'

The leader of the hunters nodded. 'My brother's scalp.'

The youngster dropped the scalp to the floor. 'No, no,' chided the old voice. 'You don't throw your shirt from you, that's made of reindeer skin. The scalp's only skin and hair, the same.'

'Reindeer don't kill and skin each other!' said the youngster.

From inside the bed came the harsh laugh. 'Only because they can't hold a knife!'

The leader of the hunters picked up the scalp and tucked it in his belt again. 'It was done by the Czar's hunters. Have you heard of the Czar, Grandmother, who says he owns all this land and even says he owns us?'

The old voice answered, sounding amused, 'I have heard some mention of this Czar.'

'Grandmother, the Czar has been sending his people into our Northlands – more and more of his people. They fish the rivers and lakes, they hunt our animals, they cut down the trees – '

'They're killing the land, Grandmother!' said another man.

The old woman's voice came whispering through the haze of candlelight and wood-dust. 'So my little daughter has been telling me.' Her ugly old hand pulled out a long strand of the girl's black hair. 'Such startling news to bring an old woman – that woodcutters are felling trees, that hunters are killing animals, and fishers are killing fish! Such shocks will be the death of me!'

The youngster, the handsome girl, said, 'Grandmother, I – ' but was quiet at once when the old woman held up a skinny hand.

There was a silence in the hot, crowded little hut. They heard the fire hissing in the stove, and the house crooning to itself.

'Grandmother,' said the hunters' leader, 'it is true that we all live by killing each other. It's the way the world turns. But always before, the hunters have left alive enough animals and trees to fill the land again; always we have sung the ghost songs, to send the ghosts safely to the Ghost World. But these hunters of the Czar, Grandmother – they don't know the ghost songs and they mean to leave nothing alive!'

'And it's not only the beavers, the foxes, the wolves they kill, either,' said another man, and others joined in.

'No – they kill our reindeer, Grandmother! Do we go to the Czar's house and steal his gold?'

There were shouts of angry agreement, and the stamping of feet.

'Yes, killed our reindeer – and when we've tried to stop them – '

'Then they've killed us!'

Another laugh came from within the bed. 'And have you never killed men of another tribe, to take their reindeer? Men have always killed each other.'

The men's excitement died away into silence. They even stopped eating.

'That's true, Grandmother,' said the leader. 'But listen – the Czar's hunters use nets of mesh so small they empty the rivers of fish, young and old. Big catches this year, none next. They cut down whole lands of trees. They catch birds in traps and they steal the eggs. And we, we who have always lived here, and hunted here, and kept our bargain with the animals – we must steal from the Czar's traps if we're to eat. And then the Czar's hunters say we are stealing from him, and shoot us!'

The old shaman said, 'A sorry story, my sons. Why do you bring it to me?'

The men had nothing to say to that. They put down their glasses. They stared at each other, and looked towards the darkness of the bed-closet.

12

The lass said quietly, 'They want you to help them, Granny.'

'And how do they think I can help?'

'Granny, my dream – '

'Shh, shh,' said the old woman, and the lass was quiet. 'Listen to me, all of you.' The shaman leaned forward in her bed, so that the candlelight fell on her, and, for the first time, the hunters saw her. She was more than old. She was a skeleton covered with wrinkled leather, worn thin. The flesh sagged from her brittle bones: the skin was crossed, recrossed and crumpled with many, many lines, both deep and fine. Age had pulled down her lower lids to show the red linings, and her eyes would not properly close. Her lips sagged away from her brown teeth, and her mouth dribbled at its ever-damp corners. A beard and moustache of fine silver hairs hung from her chin and upper lip, while her head was almost bald. Age had made her so horrible that some of the men winced at the sight of her, but the lass sitting on the bed held the old woman's hand and watched her, as she spoke, with respect and love.

'I pitied you your wanderings in this cold,' said the shaman, 'so I sent out my little falcon to find you and bring you here. And now I tell you, eat all you can, and then go back to your homes, to your people. There is no such help as you seek.'

The lass said, 'The Northlands are dying, Granny.'

'I have lived too long, more than three hundred years,' said the shaman, gasping, for she was running out of breath. 'In that time I have heard many cries of,

13

"Save us, the world is coming to an end!" But the world never was ending. It was only changing. The world must change, always, because to be unchanging is to be nothing. Even the dead change. But living things fear change and death.' She leaned from her bed towards the hunters. 'Listen to me! Neither I nor any shaman will halt this change for you, even if we could. Go back to your homes and people.' And the ancient woman lay back in the shadows of her bed-closet. They could hear her breath gasping and tearing.

The men sat at the table, not eating any more, and hanging their heads. The shadows lowered from the corners of the ceiling, and the candlelight shimmered thinly over the walls and figures like fiery water.

In the quiet came the lass's voice. 'Grandmother, I had a dream, a strong dream. I saw men coming into the Northlands, and they were all on leashes, and these leashes were all held in the hands of a man who sat on a heap of – '

'Little daughter,' said the old woman, with hardly enough breath to speak the words, and the lass stopped speaking at once. 'You are not a shaman yet. A witch – a good witch – but no shaman. So be quiet now.' The lass lowered her head. Her long black hair fell forward, starred with its white beads, and hid her face.

'You see how it is with me,' gasped the ancient woman after a while. 'I am the only shaman who will hear you, but even if I would help you, I could not. You see my little daughter here, my apprentice?' She tried to heave herself up, and the lass quickly rose and went to sit at her pillow, to lift up the old woman and support

14

her against her own shoulder. 'Three hundred years of life my own grandmother gave me when I became a shaman – and three hundred years I waited for the birth of my apprentice. I should have gone into the Ghost World long ago, but I could not leave my daughter alone . . . So on I have gone, and on, until I am nothing but clotted dust clinging to bones. My legs will not hold me up; my spine is both bent and unbending. This is my last act as a shaman before going into the Ghost World – to spare you the labour of searching any further for a shaman's help. The shamans will not help you, my sons. There is no help to give. All things must change.'

'But – ' began the leader of the men.

'But they are killing the Northlands!' rasped the old woman. 'If that is true, then you must live with the death, or you must die with it, that is all. I am going to rest now. I have a long journey ahead of me. You may eat all you want. You may even stay to see me go to the Ghost World, if you wish. Lay me down now,' she said to the lass, and the youngster carefully laid her down in the bed, before standing and closing the door of the bed-closet, to keep out draughts and the light.

The leader of the hunters stood and said, 'We shall go now.' The other men rose from their places, and they began to pull on their boots, and throw their coats and hats to each other.

'Stay, Uncles – eat more,' said the lass, but the men would not look at her or answer. They stamped their feet into their boots, pulled on their mittens, fastened coats, and they went to the door, opened it and crowded through.

A cold wind, thin but sharp, blew into the warmth of the little room, and crept round and round its corners, chilling it, as the door stayed open for the men to struggle out. But then the door clapped shut, and the draught died.

The lass went over to a window and opened a shutter a little, looking out into the grey snow-mist. She saw the shapes of the men, dim in the grey, quickly growing darker, and then vanishing altogether. She felt sadness when she could no longer see them; and she thought of them struggling home through the cold, and having nothing to tell, at the end, but how they had failed.

But they also vanish from this story (says the cat). I have no more to tell of them.

The lass returned to the bed-closet, where the hard breathing of the old shaman could be heard through the doors. She kicked a stool against the closet and sat there, dejectedly hanging her head, so her face was hidden behind her long black hair.

The door of the bed-closet was pushed open, creaking, and the voice of the old shaman said, 'You think me cruel, little daughter, but I have learned – pull one thread, and that thread pulls others, and those others pull still more. You cannot change one thing alone; you will always change many things, and you cannot tell what might become of that – it may be worse than what you tried to cure.'

The lass said, 'Grandmother, I have dreamed this same dream many times. A man – the Czar – sits on a mound of cut tree-trunks and furs and carcasses of men and animals, and in his hands he holds the leashes of many men who come here, into the Northlands. And these men, they hunt and they fish and they cut down trees. They take it all back to the Czar and make a bigger mound for him to sit on – but he sends more hunters and more, until there is nothing left beneath the stars here but snow and tree-stumps. And then they begin making more mounds, here in the Northlands, and more mounds, and more; and people come from the South to live on these mounds ... But there are no northern people left and the only animals are rats and mice and fleas ... And the new people are lonely, lonely and sick, like animals in a cage ...'

'A true dream,' said the shaman.

'But these hunters, Grandmother – the Czar holds them on leashes. They come at his orders. The Czar can order them to heel.'

'Do you think they would obey him?'

'Many would, Granny! And I am only a witch – I couldn't guard the whole of the Northlands – but I could spell one man. The Czar is only a man, isn't he? I could bind him with spells and make him call his men back. And you could do it easily, Granny. I would have to go to the Czar's city, but you, you could walk into his dreams without leaving your bed. Granny – '

The old shaman sighed with a sound like sheets tearing. 'All things must change, all things must die. I will not speak one word or sing one note to stop it.'

The lass jumped to her feet angrily and said, 'Then why have I been given this dream? What use are shamans, and what use is being a shaman?'

She lost some of her anger when the old shaman

laughed at her. 'Shamans are no use, little pancake. Shamans are like the dreamers in the Ghost World, who dream the shamans and everything else. What use are the Northlands? What use are the reindeer people? What use are trees and fish and falcons?' She lay back in her bed and gasped for breath, and the lass sat on her stool again. Then the old woman asked, 'Is my pyre built? Tonight I must go.'

The lass left her stool and threw herself down on the bed by the old woman. She lowered her head to her grandmother's shoulder, as if lying against her, as she had done when younger – but the old woman was too frail for that now: mere clotted dust and brittle bone. The lass was afraid to break her and held her weight a hair's breadth above the ancient body. The old woman put her hand on the lass's head and stroked her fingers through strands of the long black hair, enjoying, for the last time, the way its warm smoothness snagged on her fingers, both soft and coarse, like raw silk.

'You don't want me to go,' she said. 'But I've stayed too long already, and if I stay longer I shall break into pieces and blow away in the wind, and everything I was will be lost and gone. I wish . . . But what use is wishing? Still, I wish that I could have taught you the ways of the Ghost World, and made you a shaman –' Her whispering voice choked, either from weariness and lack of breath or from grief. 'When you have seen the smoke rise for me, go to my sister in the East . . . She will teach you what I've not had time to teach, and bring you to me in the Ghost World. I will be waiting for you. I will give you your three hundred years of life.'

18

The lass sat up, but her head hung and her long hair hid her face. 'You're going . . . And the land will die . . .'

The old shaman felt water fall from under the hair on to her face and arms. 'Shingebiss,' she said, using the lass's true name, 'I don't want to die, but I must. The land must die, everything must die. It is sad – but many things are sad, and if we wept for all the sad things, we would weep the seas full and flood the Earth – and when the Earth was nothing but one great drowning sea, then that would be so sad, we would have to weep again!' Breathlessly, painfully, she laughed.

Shingebiss's head hung lower, and she shook, but not with laughter.

The old shaman said, 'Now take me to my pyre.'

Shingebiss put on her heavy coat and hat and mittens, which she had not needed before when she had been clothed in warm feathers. She opened the doors of the bed-closet wide, and she went over to the house doors, and opened them, and propped them open with stools. A cold, cold wind blew into the house, and the hanging shadows climbed further down the walls as candles were blown out.

Then Shingebiss stooped over the bed and lifted the old shaman in her arms. The old woman was heavy, but Shingebiss was strong, and the weight was not too heavy. She carried the old woman across the room, and out through the door.

Out from the warmth and candlelight of the house, into the darkness, the cold, of deep winter. The wind shrilled at the house corners and struck as keen across their faces as a sharp knife-blade. The sky above was immense and black and high, freezing with stars. The white of the snow, broken by the blackness of the trees, stretched away into a grey fog of twilight, and then into deeper and deeper darkness until it met the black of the sky. Under Shingebiss's feet the frozen crust of the snow crunched and sometimes let her sink to her ankles, but held her up. The ice glittered against the white snow; the distant stars glittered against the black sky.

The pyre was close to the little house, among the trees. It had been built of bundles of branches, and its top was spread with a blanket, on which a thin layer of snow had fallen. With a last heave of her back and shoulders, Shingebiss lifted the old woman on to the pyre, and carefully laid her down. Then she ran back over the snow to the little house, and brought back the shaman's ghost drum, which she put into her hands, and a flask of drink, and a lump of smoked reindeer meat, which she laid beside the old woman.

And again Shingebiss ran back to the house, but this time she brought back, in a clay pot, fire from the stove. She climbed up on to the pyre and sat, holding the pot between her mittens, and looking at her grandmother. The freezing wind lifted her long strands of black hair and scoured her face, but still she sat there.

'Put the fire to the wood now, Shingebiss,' said the old woman.

'I'm afraid, Granny. What if I never become a shaman?'

'You are sure to, my clever lass.'

'But if I don't – how will we find each other in Iron Wood?'

The old woman reached up one arm and caught one of the long, flying plaits. Gently, she pulled Shingebiss's head down towards her and said, 'Shingebiss, there is always reason to be afraid – but whenever you poke your nose out of doors, little daughter, pack courage and leave fear at home. Do as I tell you. Go to my sister in the East, and learn from her to be a shaman. Don't love these Northlands too much, Shingebiss. Don't go to the Czar thinking you can spell him as you would a simple, sane man of the North.' She let go of the plait and held her apprentice's mittened hand while she panted for breath. 'He is only a man, the Czar – but he has a mind like broken glass, reflecting many things and all of them crookedly. I have watched him in my scrying mirror. To try spelling him would be like plunging your hand into a box of sharp knives and hooks.' She tugged Shingebiss, weakly, towards her. 'It would be dangerous to try, and if you are killed before you are made a shaman, then the Ghost World Gate will open for you only once. You will lose yourself in Iron Wood, and even if I found you there, you would not know me. Go to my sister in the East – but now get down and set the fire to the wood. I am cold up here. I want the fire!'

Shingebiss bent over and kissed her face. There were sharp spikes in the old woman's moustache and beard, which pricked, but the worn old skin was so soft that she could hardly feel it. Once the kiss was given, there was nothing more to do or say. Shingebiss climbed

21

down and set the fire to twigs in the bundles.

The cold was fierce, freezing, but dry. The twigs soon caught and blazed in the darkness. And they set light to the branches, and soon the fire leaped and roared through the bundles. Shingebiss stood back from the heat and watched the glory of the flames burning on the ice against the dark.

The old, old woman lying on the pyre was silent for a while, but soon Shingebiss heard her voice lifted above the sound of the flames and wind. She was singing a song even older than she was herself: a song which told of the journey from this world to the Ghost World, the ways which must be taken, the dangers which must be faced. As she sang, her voice weakened and faded, seeming to come from further and further away. The last words were unheard. She was at the Gate.

The pyre burned, casting flickering flares of light over the snow and drawing back to itself long shadows. The heat drove Shingebiss further away and, though it warmed her face, made the wind at her back yet more stiffeningly, cripplingly cold. Sparks, burning red, flew high against the black and silver of the sky, and the snow glared red as if stained with spilt blood. The good stink of the burning wood half choked her and drove her further off.

Shingebiss stood staring at the beauty of the fire, but, in her mind, she was the gyrfalcon again, gyring, flying. The gyrfalcon can outstare the sun. It can look down from the wing and see every pine needle, every mouse.

It can see more: it can see the harm done and the harm still to be done. It sees the trees dwindle away to cut stumps, and the city walls rear up through the snow-mist. It sees the roads dividing up the open land, leading to more cities, and it sees the foxes, the wolves, turning into fur hats and coats. It sees the traps set and the hunts riding; it hears the screams and sees the snow redden, and not with firelight. Foxes, mice, rats, fleas – these might live in cities. But not wolves, bear, lynx, beaver. Not trees.

And what use is it to be a shaman, if a shaman will do nothing?

Crippled with cold, she limped away from the dying fire into the glowing silver mist of darkness, moon and snowlight, striped and barred with the blackness of tree-trunks. All around her trees had been draped in strange cloaks and covers of snow; drifts had been blown into wind-smoothed curves, and over all glittered the hard frost.

The wind tore itself on the corners of the little house as she came to the door, and in the wind the voice of old Frost whispered, 'Are you cold, child? Are you cold?'

In the house Shingebiss found her skis, and filled a pack with food. Down from the wall she took her bow and quiver of arrows. That was all she would need for her journey to the Czar's city. She was no shaman, and never would be one. She needed no ghost drum.

Before she left she poured water on the fire in the stove and raked out the embers, so the house would die quickly. She sang it the ghost song, to tell it which way to travel, on its chicken-legs, to find her grandmother in Iron Wood.

*

And so Shingebiss goes to spell the Czar (says the cat). And while she travels, I shall tell you of this Czar, and of his city.

2

The cat walks round and round the tree, treading down the fallen leaves, clanking its golden chain.

I have many things to tell (says the cat). Forget, for a while, the lass, Shingebiss. She has a long way to go before she walks into the story again.

I must tell you (says the cat) of the man the lass hopes to spell: Ruler of the Northlands, God on Earth, the All-Powerful, the Father of his people, the Czar Grozni: a man whose mind is like a broken mirror, sharply reflecting many things, and all crookedly.

And I must tell you too of the Englishman, Richard Jenkins, and of the boy he owns.

But, before any of this, I must tell you of the Czar's city, and the Czar's palace.

A huge city it was. Tall barracks and wide parade-grounds for the Czar's soldiers, and clangorous foundries, hot even in winter, to keep the soldiers armed. Many, many offices for the Czar's clerks. Storehouses for his gold, his grain, his treasures, his papers. Prisons for his criminals and his enemies. Gallows, in the town squares, to display the bodies of criminals and the Czar's enemies; and, on every bridge, on every town gate, spikes for chopped-off heads.

Churches too: many, many churches in every part of the city. Beneath their gilded domes, in their dark interiors the candles burned, the icons glimmered and the air reeked of burning perfume, while all the priests cried, 'Obey the Czar, our God on Earth!'

And houses: street after street, lane after lane, alley after alley of houses; all with walls of wood, roofs of wood, floors and shutters and furniture all of wood. Big houses of the rich, with many wooden rooms and wooden stairs and much expensive carving; and houses smaller, and smaller still; and the huts and shacks of the poor, the cracks of windows and doors stuffed with paper and cloth against the cold.

And lovely shops, with wooden walls and glassed windows, brightly lit in the winter darkness by hissing, spluttering, high-flaring oil-lamps. Each shop smelt of the burning oil mixed with the scent of its wares: burning oil and spun sugar, burning oil and aromatic tea, burning oil and leather or, in the butchers' shops, burning oil and fresh blood.

And in the streets, even in winter, wooden market stalls were set out, and pedlars sold from wooden trays. Iron braziers full of fire stood about among the stalls, and stallholders and customers alike warmed themselves at the baskets of glowing red coals – or burning wood.

Along the river's side were wooden wharfs to receive the wooden ships that came every day, and wooden warehouses to store the goods they brought. Poor men unloaded things they could never afford to buy: tea, silk, amber, perfume, ingots of silver and gold. They loaded them on to wooden carts and they were hauled away into the city, over roads made of wooden blocks.

And through every wooden gate of the city – beneath the spiked heads of the Czar's enemies – passed more wooden carts, loaded with fresh and salted fish in wooden barrels, with live fowls in wooden cages, and, even in winter, wooden baskets of fresh vegetables and fruit.

A vast, gobbling city, the Czar's city, drawing to itself and gobbling all that the land can produce: fruit, grain, vegetables, meat, furs, timber, iron, salt, gold, coal – oh, more things than I could list or you could hear.

But, more than anything, wood. The city was built of wood, and, unlike the felled trees, the city was forever growing. Thousands of trees had been felled to raise the city, and thousands more were cut as the city grew – whole forests were cleared and dragged into the city to lie in trees' graveyards as the dead wood was mummified for use. Every wall, every fence, every door, every window-frame, every cart axle, every bucket, every bowl and every spoon, every stool, every clog, every toothpick, meant another dead tree.

And at the centre of this shining, noisy, stinking city was another city, surrounded by a high wall of stone, not wood, so it could not be burned or hacked down. The city behind that stone wall was the Czar's palace.

The palace was not one building, but many. It had its own streets, squares, yards, burying grounds and pleasure gardens. There were workshops for the making of clothes in fur and silk and cloth of gold; workshops for jewellers, goldsmiths, silversmiths, blacksmiths; for carpenters and joiners; for coach-makers, for painters, for upholsterers, for gilders and glass-cutters and instrument-makers. There were gardeners to take care of the pleasure gardens, to keep the fountains flowing and feed the caged birds – but in winter, the fountains were frozen and the birds had been taken in from the killing cold.

There were barracks for the Czar's guards, and coach-houses, and stables, kennels and slave-quarters. There were vast kitchens where banquets were prepared, and the hundreds of dishes and bowls and glasses washed afterwards. There were offices where clerks worked to organize it all and never quite succeeded; there were laundries and bakeries and slaughterhouses, dairies and breweries. And there were houses for these workers to live in, and halls where they could gather to eat.

Nor was that all. There were grander apartments for visiting nobles, and schoolrooms for their children. There were rehearsal rooms for the Czar's musicians, singers and dancers; and there was a small theatre where they would perform.

There were the state apartments: the throne room, where the Czar held court and gave judgement; the great dining hall where he could dine with all his nobles at once if he wished; ballrooms as long as a city street; council chambers. There were libraries where thousands of books were stored and never read; and where the records of the law cases, and rents, and taxes were kept, and read constantly. And then there were the private apartments of the Czar.

And the churches. Though there were so many churches in the outer city, the Czar had still more within his wall. The royal church, where the Czar attended service with his family and nobles, and where every inch of the walls and ceiling was painted with saints in gold, green, scarlet, blue and yellow. There were smaller churches for the soldiers, even churches of different, heathen faiths for the foreign soldiers in the Czar's guard: the English and Scots, the Greeks and Turks, the Mongols and Swedes. There were chapels for women, and chapels for slaves, special chapels for musicians and singers, and even a little chapel where the Czar's cows, horses, mules, donkeys, cats and dogs might be taken, to hear service and be blessed in their endless labours.

Early every morning, when the gates of the Czar's palace opened, there would already be a long queue outside, of carts and horses and men, waiting to bring into the palace the fruit, the wood, the milk, grain, meat, water, charcoal, and everything and anything else that might be needed. All day long, until the gates were closed again at night, the carts and the people and the animals went in and out, with a rolling noise of iron-edged wheels and iron-shod hooves on the logs that paved the roadway. And from inside the palace came servants sent on errands, soldiers off duty, nobles riding out to see the town.

But even here, in the city, and even in the palace yards, old Granddad Frost rode his sharp-backed horse, leaning from it to whisper, 'Are you cold, children? Are you cold?' And with his long white nails, he scratched at the people's skin until it glowed red. Red faces everywhere, beneath hats and scarves: cheeks, noses, scratched red by the cold. Here and there a nose grown too cold gleamed white, and then passers-by cried, 'Rub your nose, rub your nose – Father Frost is *biting* you!'

And over the whole city, even in the palace yards, the snow fell, sifting down slowly and silently from above, its whiteness shining in the dark and vanishing in the light from windows, hissing into burning braziers, covering dirt with white, outlining tiles and planks until the whole city seemed made of snow.

And above all, above all, the black, black sky leaned down with its weight of silver stars.

Leave the freezing yards, and pass through the doors of the palace, and you pass into more darkness and a deep silence. The thick walls – built thick against the cold – hushed the din of the palace yards, and the coming and going of carts and people, hushed it to a drone, a murmur. And inside the palace there was no noise except for the faint breath of burning candles, the brush of a soft shoe on a floor of polished wood. This was the house of the Czar, the God on Earth, and, to show respect for him, no one might speak aloud. They might whisper, if they had to, but whispers carry in long, silent corridors, and so it was safer not to speak at all. There was no laughter in the palace, only hidden smiles. A soldier who dropped his pike with a startling clatter, a maid who let fall a jug with a crash, would be whipped.

The windows of the palace were not of clear glass, but of stone cut to paper thinness, and painted with symbols: the three Holy Golden Crowns; the scarlet Imperial Eagle and the Black Bear; the green leaves and scarlet flowers of the Tree of Life. They let through little light. On the brightest summer's day the light in the palace rooms and corridors was a cool twilight, stained rose and emerald by the Tree of Life, or gold and azure by the Holy Crowns, or blotched with the black shape of the Bear. In winter, the palace held a deep, cool, silent darkness. Here and there in the long, dim corridors there was a room lit to a hot, golden blaze by many, many clusters of burning candles, but even the brightest candlelight was dim and flickering; even in the brightest candlelit room you had to peer and squint.

In the Czar's palace were many, many mansions, many houses, many rooms. There were candlelit staircases, wide as streets, leading up to splendid balconies; and there were narrow, all but dark steps leading to attics and cellars. There were passages and bridges joining one building to another; there were towers, there were tunnels; there were hundreds of doors which, if opened, might reveal a hall panelled in sheets of amber, an airing cupboard, a dressing-room like a little trinket-box, or a stinking privy.

Come (says the cat), come deep into this palace maze, deep into this jewel-lit twilight, this silence: climb this stair, go through this door, across this freezing yard, around this corner. Open this door. Look in. What, and whom, do you see?

A large room, long and high, its windows shuttered against the outer dark and cold. Two tall, heavy bronze stands of candles gave the only light. Red and gold, the candlelight licked over the bronze, and candle-grease had hung the stands with white stalactites. But only the centre of the room was touched by the golden light and heat of the candles: shabby darkness hid the ceiling above, hid the distant walls and corners. Wafting from that darkness, carrying scents of wood and dust, came slight, cool breezes that made the candles waver and the shadows jump on the walls.

On the floor near the candlestand a room-wide circle had been thickly drawn in white chalk which gleamed in the light. At the circle's four quarters stood iron braziers filled with hot red coals that added a dull red tinge to the light, and to the room a stink and sound of burning.

Inside the circle stood a table draped with a black cloth. On it, a white-handled knife, a sword, several small dishes of coloured powders, and a flask of wine.

Across the circle from the table stood a large wooden chair. Each of its arms was supported by a carved bear, and its back was carved with the three Holy Crowns, their gilding glimmering in the candlelight.

Outside the circle, where the candlelight edged into darkness, two figures stood in talk, a man and a devil. The man was short but wide, with broad shoulders and a thick neck, and a large, round belly. His dark robe almost covered his slippered feet and was plain except for a trimming of fur. He held a carved staff, as tall as himself, in one large, thick-fingered hand. His round face was plump-cheeked, and the candlelight cast deep shadows around the folds of flesh under his eyes and at the sides of his mouth, though his grey beard hid the sagging flesh under his chin. His hair was thick and grey, and grew in a frizzy, curly ruff around his bald head. The red light from the braziers couldn't, alone, have made his nose and cheeks so red. This (says the cat) was Master Richard Jenkins, an Englishman and a wizard.

The devil was a red and furry devil, its fur rippling in the candlelight like red velvet. Its tail had an arrow's point on the end, and was long, and coiled and bounced like a spring as the devil moved. Its head was fearsome, large and round with staring, glittering eyes and ram's horns; and all around its head and shoulders hung a shimmering red mist.

'Are you listening to me?' said Master Jenkins to the devil – in English. 'Take off the head when I talk to you!' The devil, with much struggling and jiggling, wrenched off its tight-fitting head. Underneath was another: the head of a boy. His brown eyes blinked in the candles' smoke, and his cropped fair hair stood up in tufts. He clutched the devil's head in his velvet-suited arms, and fingered the wire spikes, hung with strings of red sequins, that decorated it. These sequined spikes, and others projecting from his shoulders, trembled in the light and made the red mist around him. This devil (says the cat) is named Christian. He is a very obedient devil, because he is much smaller and thinner than Master Jenkins, and he is afraid of him.

'I hope you've been listening,' said Master Jenkins. 'Important matters, these. I don't want everything going wrong because you've missed your cues.' As an afterthought, he gave Christian's head a meaty clout.

Christian hung his head and looked away from his master into the darkness.

'Well – did you hear what I said?'

'Master – I'm frightened, Master,' Christian said – and that he dared to say it was a measure of how scared he was. 'Do we – do you think we should do this, Master?'

'Why do you think we've been rehearsing, you idiot? And what business is it of yours?' Christian hung his head again, lower than before. 'Keep your mouth shut and stop interrupting. All you have to do is what you're told – and get it right, do you hear? Get it right or I'll warm you. Now – what's your first cue?'

The question took Christian by surprise, and he could not think of the answer, or of anything. The silence drew out, and he knew that Master Jenkins would not wait for long, but the more nervous he became, the less he could think. And dunt! went Master Jenkins's hand against his head, setting his brain-pan humming. Tears filled his eyes, and he began to tremble, for fear that worse was coming.

'No snivelling!' said Master Jenkins. 'You've nowt to be frit of *if* you remember your cues – or, if you must be frit of something, be frit of *me*! Now, your first cue?'

Christian swallowed tears, sniffed snot up his nose, and said miserably, 'I am in the cupboard . . .'

'Aye, aye, the cupboard – '

'And I have the strings in my hand – '

'Don't drop them or pull them too soon!'

'No, Master. I am in the cupboard, and you are saying all the words – '

'Aye, but your cue, you idiot-born *Dummkopf*?'

'I wait and keep quiet until you say . . . ah . . . until you say . . .' Still the right answer wouldn't come into his head and Christian couldn't help but look nervously at Master Jenkins's hand, which was lifting into the air.

'You say – '

'I say *what*?'

'Ah . . . ah . . . Don't hit, I'll remember! Ah – "Pleasant form!" . . . ah . . . "Appear to us, not in thy true shape, but in some pleasant form!"' Master Jenkins lowered his hand, so Christian knew he had it right. 'And that's – *is* that when I ring the bell, Master?'

Master Jenkins glowered. 'Well? *Is* it when you ring the bell?'

Christian's eyes wandered from his master's face to the burning candles behind him, and the blackness beyond. He knew from Master Jenkins's tone that if he answered this question wrongly, he would get more than a clout on the head. 'That's when I ring the bell.' He started to duck.

'That is when you ring the bell,' said Master Jenkins, and Christian felt warm and weak with relief.

Master Jenkins's hard, bruising forefinger prodded him in the chest. 'Don't pull the string for the thunder-sheet instead! Remember that! And after you've rung the bell, then what?'

Christian's face twisted unhappily. However much he managed to remember, there was always more. 'Then . . . you throw the powders into the fire and make a lot of smoke . . .'

'Aye? Then?'

'And you say, "Do us no harm, I command thee, by the Trinity, by the Virgin, come, appear!"'

'Hmm,' said Master Jenkins, and reached out his hand. Christian flinched from it, but Master Jenkins only patted his shoulder and said, 'You have learned that line well.'

Indeed Christian had, as it seemed like a protecting prayer, to protect him from Master Jenkins, and both of them from the Czar. But he was so glad not to be hit, and so pleased by this praise from his master, that he blushed, and hung his head, unable to stop his face smiling foolishly. Hoping for more praise, he went on quickly, 'And then I pull the thunder-sheet's string and make a din –'

'Aye, good, and then?'

'And then you say, Master, "Come, oh, come, Oh spirit! Come, oh, come!" And you throw the thunder-flash in the fire, and I come out of the cupboard . . . kee-keeping hold of the thunder-sheet string –'

'But you must not pull it.'

'No, I must not pull it yet. Then I dance around, being a devil. I have my squealer.' He showed Master Jenkins the pipe in his hand, which would change his voice when he fitted it behind his teeth. 'And then –'

Master Jenkins suddenly raised his arm, and Christian flinched again, but his master only dropped his arm, like a hot, heavy stole, around Christian's shoulders. 'Good, very good, Christy. You've learned that all very well. You'll remember the rest.'

Christian began to tremble more because Master Jenkins's arm was round him, and because he wasn't sure at all that he could remember the rest. If he didn't, Master Jenkins would beat his back and arms and legs as well as his head. 'I'm not sure, Master, I'm not sure – '

'Of course you will. We haven't time to go through it all again. You have to put on the head and get into the cupboard.'

More tears filled Christian's eyes and he began to shake harder. He hated wearing the head, which was so heavy and made it hard to breathe and hear. He hated being in the small cupboard, where time passed so slowly, until he was sure he had missed all his cues. And now he couldn't remember his first cue any more, and all the other cues had vanished into a darkness of fright. All he could remember was Master Jenkins's rages, the pain of past beatings, and the misery of being kept hungry. 'Please, Master, please go through it again . . . I'm not sure . . . do you think I'll forget some of it, Master? I want to get it right.'

Master Jenkins leaned his face close to Christian's and said, 'If you think you might make a mistake, just remember that the Czar will be here!'

Christian had been so worried by Master Jenkins, who was in front of him, close enough to strike a blow, that he had forgotten the Czar. Now horrible, bright, wordless pictures danced in his head: the Czar, pulling off his devil's head and discovering that he was only a boy. The Czar's executioner cracking his whip, the back-breaking knout. His own head, and Master Jenkins's, stuck side by side on spikes, while their bodies hung on gallows in the next street. He stared at Master

Jenkins, frozen, with tears running down his face.

'Listen,' Master Jenkins said, 'don't worry about the Czar.' He leaned close to Christian, lowered his voice to a whisper and couldn't stop himself from quickly looking round. 'The Czar is a fool!' Again he looked round the empty room. 'We've proved that he's a fool often enough. I could present you to him stark naked in broad daylight, tell him you were a green-mustachioed Finnish badger, and he'd believe it.' Christian tried to smile at the joke, and Master Jenkins took the devil's head from his arms. 'There are two kinds of folk in the world, Christy. Folk who tell lies and folk who believe lies. We tell them, the Czar believes. But there's no point in making it harder for him to believe than we have to, so get it right! Think of my belt and my fist – that'll help you concentrate!' He put the devil's head over Christian's and forced it down by pulling and twisting on the ram's horns. 'Now, into the cupboard. Hurry up!'

The walls of the room were panelled in wood, and one of the panels stood open. It led into a narrow, dark space between the panelling and the outer wall. A cold breeze blew from the opening. Christian made sure that his devil's head was firmly on and, quivering with fright, slipped through the opening and into the space. The wires on the devil's head and shoulders caught on the edge of the panelling for a moment, and Master Jenkins kicked him on the leg, to help him free the wires and get inside. Once Christian was inside, Master Jenkins waited impatiently until he had taken into his hands the strings that operated the bell and the thunder-sheet. Then he closed the panel and shut his frightened apprentice into the cold, narrow darkness where he was to wait, keeping quite still and quite silent, clutching the strings in his stiff fingers, for an endless time.

Once closed, the door in the panelling vanished. It was so hard to see that even Master Jenkins, who had built it, sometimes had to search the panelling with his fingernails for minutes before finding it.

Master Jenkins, humming to himself, made ready for the arrival of the Czar. First he moved the stands of candles a little further from the hidden door, so that no gleam of candlelight should reveal it. Next he checked the table and his bowls of powders. He was dusting the great wooden chair when he heard the tramp of marching feet approaching across the yard, and then mounting the wooden steps to the door. The door was shaken by a banging fist, and a voice yelled, 'Open in the name of the Czar!'

Master Jenkins hurried to the double doors and opened them. In came black-clothed soldiers, armed with pikes, who spread quickly throughout the room, searching it for the Czar's enemies. Master Jenkins didn't watch them. He doubted whether they were bright enough to find the hidden cupboard, but if they found it, they found it, and watching them would only help them find it sooner. Instead, as the Czar entered, Master Jenkins went to his belly and lay flat, to show his deep respect.

The Czar came striding in, his eyes already darting about the room to watch his soldiers, whom he didn't trust. He paused for a moment and looked down from his tall height at Master Jenkins lying on the ground. With the toe of his boot he touched him and said, 'Rise, Jyenkinz.' This was a great honour. Master Jenkins was almost the only person alive whom the Czar trusted – a little.

The Czar trusted no one fully because he feared, always, that someone was planning his murder. So he feared to be alone and unprotected, but he also feared to be in crowds, where many people who meant him harm might be gathered together. Perhaps most of all he feared the future, which was like a long dark corridor, with an even deeper darkness at its further end. In this dark corridor, into which he must go, assassins and attackers might be waiting at every step. The Czar hoped that Master Jenkins's predictions would be a lamp to light the way along that fearful, dark corridor of future time – and so he trusted Master Jenkins. A little.

And what was the Czar like? He was taller and thinner than most men. His hair hung far below his shoulders and his beard fell to his waist, but both beard and hair were dirty, hanging in greasy, twisted strings, and it was impossible to tell, by the dim light of the candles, whether it was dark or fair. He wore a long, sombre kaftan which covered him from throat to foot, its long sleeves hiding his hands. The cloth was stitched with much twining, intricate embroidery, but the frail candlelight seemed to sink into the robe's dark colours and nothing of the pattern could be seen clearly. Only the robe's gems showed, glittering like frost at the Czar's every movement, at every flicker of flame. The gems glittered as the Czar, his robes swinging to his stride, passed by Master Jenkins and entered the chalk circle.

Master Jenkins was struggling to get up from the floor. He knew enough to hold his breath as the stinking breeze of the Czar's passing enclosed him. It was the custom in the Czar's country to bathe at least once a week, but it was not the Czar's custom, and he stank of sweat and urine as rankly as a cage where a large beast has been kept. Trying hard to look as if he had smelt a sweet smell of roses, Master Jenkins used his hands to push himself to his knees, and then awkwardly, breathlessly, clambered to his feet. Once on his feet, he found himself being jostled by the Czar's followers – more black-clothed soldiers, and many lords who wore their hair in long curls and were all dressed in kaftans of bright brocades, whose colours flared as they neared the candles and faded as they passed them.

Among these lords, Master Jenkins recognized one or two. There was the father and son from one of the Czar's far northern cities. They had visited Master Jenkins, but secretly, and now he pretended not to know them, and they never gave him a glance.

And then there was Lord Pavel, a handsome young man who always had a smile on his face, so well pleased with himself was he. He thought too well of himself to notice Master Jenkins, who was low-born and a foreigner. But Master Jenkins took a good look at young Lord Pavel, who, so he had been told, had called him a fraud, a trickster and a fairground magician. Well,

41

my little lord, thought Master Jenkins, we shall see what you say after today.

The Czar had seated himself in the wooden chair, and Master Jenkins dropped to his knees in front of it, so that his head should not be higher than his Imperial master's. 'Great Czar, do not punish me but give me permission to speak.'

The Czar, sitting with his chin resting on one hand, did not look at Master Jenkins, but muttered something unheard with a twist of his mouth. He seemed to say, 'Get on with it.'

'Great Czar, I purpose to raise demon. All people must in circle stand. In circle is safe. Out circle, not safe, Great Czar. Demon will tear to scraps all people out of circle!'

This caused some head-turning among the black-clothed soldiers, and even among the lords. The lords all edged forward until they were crammed inside the circle, but the soldiers, who were stationed around the walls of the room, did not dare to move until they were given permission.

'Great Czar, your soldiers – '

'Can stay where they are,' said the Czar. His voice was loud and carrying even when he did not mean to shout. The soldiers stiffened to attention where they stood. 'Let the demon tear them.' His eyes moved from one soldier to another. 'I have plenty of soldiers.'

'Great Czar, as you will.' Master Jenkins bowed his head. 'Great Czar, suffer me standing to be – ' He took an impatient flick of the Czar's hand for permission and climbed to his feet.

'I begin ceremony,' he said.

From his table he took up a silver bowl of water and a small silver sprinkler, and he moved about the circle, sprinkling water from the bowl in all parts of it, splashing the kneeling lords, and even daring to splash the Czar, as he said, 'I bless this circle and sanctify it in the name of the Holy, Spotless Virgin, of the Father, the Son and the Holy Ghost. I invoke the power of the Holy Trinity to make its walls safe against all the powers of Hell.' He spoke in English, which the Czar and his lords didn't understand, and which Master Jenkins hoped sounded mysterious and magical.

Returning to the table, he replaced the bowl and sprinkler, and took up the white-handled knife. He also, secretly, snatched a little powder from one of the bowls before raising the knife in the air and walking slowly about the circle. At the first brazier, he said, 'Gracious spirits of the North, of Ice and Wind and Darkness, guard us now from the one who comes . . .' His voice rose powerfully and died away in the corners of the room with muffled, woody echoes.

Some of the soldiers, outside the protection of the circle, were already pale and quivering with the effort of staring straight before them and not into the shadows. Too quick to be seen, Master Jenkins dropped a pinch of powder into the hot coals of the first brazier, and paced on to the next. Behind him, greenish smoke began to spill heavily from the coals, darkening the already dark room.

But, by then, everyone was watching Master Jenkins at the next brazier. 'Good spirits of the East, of Sunrise

and Morning and Spring, guard us, we pray thee . . .'
Another little pinch of powder dropped into that
brazier, and Master Jenkins went on to the next. Even
the Czar was sitting straighter in his chair and listening
closely. The kneeling lords were very still.

'Noble spirits of the South, of Fire and Something or
Other (it doesn't matter because they don't understand
me), give us your protection . . .' In the dark, inside the
hidden cupboard, Christian faintly heard his master's
joke and felt sick with fright. He moved his fingers to
feel the strings in them, afraid that he had dropped
them. His heart hammered in the horribly empty space
in his chest, and he truly thought he would spew inside
his demon's head . . .

'Spirits of the West, of Sunset and Rain, guard us
from the one who comes . . .' By now, smoke had drifted
in front of the candles. Nothing certain could be seen.
The smoke smelt strong and unpleasant. To breathe it
was to feel a band tighten around the head.

Master Jenkins returned to the centre of the circle,
just in front of the Czar's chair, and held the knife
upright between his two hands. 'Come to me, Hell-
dweller! Come, I summon thee, spirit of the Hell-pit:
come, come!'

Master Jenkins kissed the knife and sheathed it,
returning it to the table as he picked up the sword with
a flourish – and, without a flourish, some powder. He
went to stand in front of the northern brazier, held the
sword before him, and shouted, 'I command thee, Hell-
thing, in the name of Jesu, our Saviour, by the Father,
by the Holy Ghost, come to us now, appear to us, not in

thy true shape, but in some pleasant form – '

Through the smoky, choking, impenetrable darkness came the jangling of a bell. A thump followed as a soldier fainted and fell. The Czar straightened in his chair, a hand gripping each wooden arm, his head fully erect and staring into the smoke.

'Come to us!' cried Master Jenkins, making everyone jump again. The candlelight was smothered, but the braziers glowed red through the smoke. 'Do us no harm, I command thee, by the Trinity, by the Virgin, do us no harm. Come! Appear!'

The air of the room, the very walls, suddenly seemed to shudder and groan aloud – a reverberating, rolling thunderclap sounded – within walls! – and went rolling on and on. The Czar started up from his seat and stood staring into the air, though he could see nothing but rolling clouds of smoke. There was another thump as another soldier fainted, and the sound of Master Jenkins coughing.

'You are close, I know you are close. Come, oh, come, Oh spirit!' cried Master Jenkins, as the thunder faded. 'Come, oh, come!' And he threw the powder he held into the fire, quickly stepped back and turned aside his head with closed eyes.

A brilliant white flash lit clouds of smoke, as a lightning flash lights a thundercloud, and seared away all sight. Christian shoved hard at the door of his cupboard, pushing it open with a bang. Out he sprang into the smoke, with a ring of the bell and another rumble of thunder. He dropped the string that rang the bell, and shook his wrist to slacken the thunder-sheet string wrapped around it, and then he danced and pranced and spun, and every heavy beat of his heart made him feel more sick and more scared.

The soldiers saw him through the smoke, saw a dim, dancing misshapen thing that glimmered with a red glow even in that gloom, and they pressed close to the walls behind them. They believed that they were seeing a devil come up out of Hell, and they didn't want it to know they were there.

The Czar and his lords, peering through watering, smoke-stung eyes still dazzled by the flash, peering through the clouds of smoke that still hung in the air, saw something that had a monstrous head, and a red, hellish light shimmering about it . . . It had a tail, certainly, that coiled and bobbed jauntily behind it . . . and its upper body and arms seemed to undulate and twist in a most inhuman fashion . . . Master Jenkins heard gasps from the Czar and the lords, and a sudden rattle of rosary beads, and he smiled. Good little Christian: he was a good little devil after all.

'You are at my command, evil creature!' Master Jenkins cried, so fiercely that Christian, hearing his master's voice angry, started and shrank back from the edge of the circle. But if anyone in the room was relieved to see how afraid the devil was of their wizard, their feelings were changed in the next instant, when the devil screamed and rushed forward to the edge of the circle, its clawed feet shushing and clicking on the wooden floor, the red mist scintillating about its misshapen head. It grunted, it chattered, it twittered, in a most eerie and unnerving way, and reached out its clawed hands towards them. The kneeling lords began to feel that they were too close to the edge of the circle, and shuffled on their knees towards its centre, jostling against each other and bickering in frightened whispers.

'The circle make us safe from you,' said Master Jenkins sternly, in the Czar's language. 'Is a holy circle. I command you, speak in language we understand. Speak, and answer questions.'

The demon screeched out, in a strange, clacking, shrill voice, 'Ask! Ask!' And it prowled the edge of the circle.

'The Great Czar wish to know,' said Master Jenkins, 'who is his enemy?'

The demon laughed jerkily in its strange, harsh, squeaky voice. 'I tell you your friend, Czar!' it said, and it danced forward and reached for Master Jenkins who, confident in the power of his magic circle, did not flinch. 'This man is your friend – I would tear him to pieces if I could! This man is your friend – all others your enemies!'

The Czar stood quite still.

'And what of future time, demon?' asked Master Jenkins. 'Do you have advice for future?'

'Grant the wishes of the men from the North,' screeched the demon. 'Grant their wishes and good will come of it. Refuse them, and –' The demon laughed, screeching and shrilling with an unbearable sound. Another soldier fainted and thudded to the floor.

'One more question, demon,' said Master Jenkins.

'Great Czar, he wish for Elixir of Life. Tell me how to make.'

'No, no, no!' the demon screamed. 'Is not for mortals! It can never be revealed!'

'Demon, I command you!' cried Master Jenkins, raising his sword once more – but his voice was lost in thunder; and there was another blinding lightning flash. In the noise and the flash, Christian skipped nimbly back into his cupboard and, gripping a hand-hold on the inside of the door, yanked it hard so that it shut with a bang, and was hidden in the panelling again. Once inside, with a slight scratching of his wires on the wood, he sank weakly to his knees, held his hand to his painfully beating heart, and swallowed down sickness.

'Demon, demon, return, I command you!' Master Jenkins yelled in English. 'I order you, in the name of the Trinity, in the name of Mary, maiden and mother, come back, come back!'

But Christian remained in his cupboard, as Master Jenkins had told him to do.

Master Jenkins dropped on to his knees. 'Great Czar, forgive me. I not strong as demon. I cannot hold it – it has gone.'

The Czar slowly seated himself in his chair again. He stared before him, at the clouds of smoke that still drifted thinly across the candles. In the gloom that hung over the further end of the room, he could see the slumped bodies of his soldiers on the floor.

'I will try again, to make demon tell me secret of Elixir, Great Czar. Forgive me that I could not this time!'

48

The Czar waved his hand, dismissing that matter. 'You are my only friend, foreigner?' he said.

'Great Czar . . . The words of a demon . . . But my circle compel it to tell truth . . . Certainly I am friend of Czar, but only friend . . .?' Master Jenkins shrugged.

'And the northern lords are to have their wishes?' the Czar said, glancing to the left of his chair, where knelt the lords from the northern city. They quickly lowered their eyes and stared intently at the floor.

Someone to the right of the chair said, 'Great Czar, do not punish me but give me permission to speak.' Master Jenkins quickly snatched round his head, and was not pleased to see that the speaker was Lord Pavel.

And the Czar nodded, granting permission to the wretch.

'Great Czar,' said Pavel, 'you are too wise to listen to the advice of this Englishman and his demon. Consider, Czar – why is the room so dark, and filled with so much smoke? Why does Jyenkinz throw powder into the fire and make a bright flash? Why, so we don't see his accomplice come out of hiding, dressed as a devil . . . I know my Czar is too wise to listen to the lies of an Englishman.'

The Czar said nothing, but stared away into the shadows of the long room.

The older of the northern lords said, 'Great Czar, forgive me for speaking – but what of the bell we all heard ring, where no bells are? What of the thunder we heard? Are these English lies?'

Pavel smiled. 'Northerners, Czar, are as simple as the English are cunning. There is a bell hidden somewhere, sir, with a string to pull it by – and a thunder-sheet, such as the Czar has in his theatre. Either Master Jyenkinyz is pulling these strings himself, or his accomplice is. Simple trickery – you may see it done in a dark tent at any fair. As you know, of course, Great Czar.'

Christian, hidden in his cupboard, could not hear these words, since they were not shouted. So Christian was spared the fear Master Jenkins felt. But Master Jenkins knew better than to show any dismay or fear. He merely lifted up his chubby head and smiled a little.

'And why,' Pavel asked, 'did the demon not tear the soldiers to pieces? When Master Jyenkinz wished to clear as many witnesses from the room as possible, he threatened that it would tear to pieces anyone outside the circle. But what did it do, this fearsome demon? It danced, it squeaked, and went away without doing harm to any – just as if it were a boy in costume! May I ask, Master Jyenkinz, where is your serving-boy? Could he not bring us wine?'

Master Jenkins decided it best to ignore these questions. He tilted up his chin, and looked away from Pavel, as if he were too proud to answer.

Then the Czar spoke. 'My Elixir?' he said, to Master Jenkins.

Master Jenkins was quick to answer *him*. 'Great Czar, it will take much work – much work! – to force secret from demon. Many, many books – much labour – but I shall have secret in end.'

'Captain!' the Czar yelled, and the black-clothed Captain of his Guard (who had managed to keep from fainting) came hurrying across the room. 'Arrest him,' said the Czar, pointing.

And the soldier arrested the lord Pavel, who, in his annoyance at Master Jenkins, had been much too careless in his choice of words. He had suggested that the Czar had been deceived by a fairground trickster, and to suggest that the Czar could ever be wrong was treason. The sentence for treason was a public death, followed by the display of the traitor's severed head on the gates of the palace; and the traitor's body to be cut in four pieces, and hung in the city's four quarters.

Master Jenkins made his face serious as Pavel was taken from the room by the guards. He didn't want anyone to remember him smiling at such a thing. But inside he smiled. He had known that the Czar would believe him. He knew that the more thoroughly anyone proved him to be a trickster, the more firmly the Czar would believe in him – because the Czar was a fool, and fools always believe the greatest lie they hear, and refuse to believe the truth, however plainly it is set before their eyes. What a silly boy Pavel was to think otherwise, and what a silly boy Christian was to fear discovery!

The Czar rose to his feet and a strong reek of sweat came from his filthy, bejewelled silken robes, which he had worn and slept in for many days. He stood silent for a long time, his head lowered, the candlelight shining oilily on the greasy tangles of his hair, and sharply on the broken ends of golden embroidery threads. The light shone on his long nose, and long cheekbones, and made deep black holes of his eyes.

Master Jenkins went on kneeling, as did the lords, patiently waiting for the Czar to speak. They dared do nothing else.

Then the Czar lifted his head and looked at Master Jenkins. The red light of the brazier fires lit only the underside of the Czar's face, and the dim, flickering light of the candles was so poor that Master Jenkins could not see the Czar's expression. The Czar's eyes were still mere hollows of blackness; and the shadows cast by the large Imperial nose and the Imperial beard hid the twist of the mouth. But the whole shadowed cast of the face was not reassuring, and Master Jenkins felt his heart squeeze small inside him.

Oh God, he knows, thought Master Jenkins. He *knows*. And despite his comfortable thoughts of a few moments before, his heart began to beat uncomfortably fast, and he sweated lightly all over.

Master Jenkins had good reason to know that the Czar was a fool. But, as Master Jenkins also knew too well, there is no one so angry as a fool when he discovers that he is a fool. And when the angry fool is a Czar who entertains his people with day-long executions, then the trickster may be sure of unhappiness when he is caught out.

But the Czar said only, 'I shall go and pray.' As Master Jenkins bowed deeply, more from relief than respect, the Czar went from the room, another sweat-scented breeze gusting from his robes. A tiny clattering, of something small falling on to the wooden floor, followed him as he went. The lords all rose from their knees and followed after him, and after them went the soldiers.

Once the door had closed behind them all, and the sound of their feet had died away, Master Jenkins sucked in a long breath, sighed with thankfulness, and stood still for a moment, hugging himself with pleasure because he was still whole. The Czar was still the Czar of Fools! He looked carefully about the room, to make sure that the black-clothed soldiers had taken all their fainting colleagues with them. He took a candle from the stand, stood it in a bowl from his table, and walked all about the room, lighting all the corners, to make doubly sure that no one had remained behind.

As he searched, he remembered the tiny sounds of something falling from the Czar's robes, and he took his candle back to the chalk circle and, bending double, shone its light over the wooden floor. He spotted, by their glitter, three jewels that had fallen from the broken threads on the Czar's robe: two rubies and an emerald. Carefully gathering them into his palm, Master Jenkins walked back towards the other end of the room. As he passed the place where Christian was closed in the hidden cupboard, he hesitated – but then looked at the jewels in his hand and hurried on. It was better to leave Christian in the cupboard. He wouldn't dare come out until Master Jenkins told him he could.

Lighting his way with the tall candle, Master Jenkins passed through a door at the far end of the room and at once began to climb a narrow, dark staircase. The candle shifted the darkness ahead of him, but it fell back behind him. At the top, the candlelight shone glossily on the panels of another door and, opening it,

Master Jenkins passed into a much smaller room than the one he had left downstairs.

The candlelight made a wavering stripe along the length of a dark wooden table, polished by use rather than wax. When Master Jenkins lifted his candle, the light spun up the walls and across the ceiling before steadying on the cases of books that lined one wall. Important, solemn books they were, with thick leather covers, and iron clasps to hold them shut. Some even had locks. The books had such titles as *The Princes of Hell and Their Legions*, *Greyskin*, *Saemund's Grimoire* and *Merlin's Book*. Every one of them was a book of black magic.

As Master Jenkins walked through the room towards another door on the other side, the light of his candle rippled over shelves of fragile glass pipes and crucibles, and shone on cold stone mortars and pestles. It lit on bunches of dried herbs hanging from the ceiling, and the shadows cast by them circled round as Master Jenkins approached, passed underneath them and walked away, carrying the light with him.

The light lit up labels on jars and phials, which read, 'Tears Wept by the Image of the Black Madonna', 'Baby's Fat', 'Crocodile Dung', 'Moss from the Skull of a Hanged Man', before the candlelight passed by and they fell into darkness again. None of the jars (says the cat) held what their labels claimed they held. The crocodile dung was horse dung from the palace stables. The baby's fat was lard from the palace kitchens. The moss from a hanged man's skull was scraped from the stones around one of the palace fountains. And the tears wept by the image of the Black Madonna had been wept by

Christian – who shed more tears, with more reason, than any image of the Madonna ever made.

Master Jenkins opened the door at the further end of this cluttered storeroom, and passed through into a room both brightly lit and warm. This was Master Jenkins's private room, and he was well satisfied with it.

The wooden shutters were fastened across the windows, and curtains of red velvet were drawn across the shutters, closing out the winter dark and cold. A stove, decorated with blue and white tiles, radiated heat into the room and made it so hot that the wooden walls creaked and released a faint forest scent. Close to the stove was a comfortable, cushioned chair, with a footstool before it. An oil-lamp on a stand stood behind the chair, to give a light for Master Jenkins to read by, and beside the chair was a low table, crowded with things: a closed book with a silken bookmark, a plate of cakes, a cut lemon, a tea-glass in a holder, and another oil-lamp. Next to the table was a silver samovar, standing on eagle's claws, with an eagle's screaming head for a tap.

Master Jenkins's bed was on the other side of the room, hidden by the red velvet curtains that Christian had drawn around it after making it. (Christian slept on the floor in the storeroom.) On a table beside the bed was another oil-lamp, so that Master Jenkins could read before he went to sleep.

More books hid the walls. The shelves which would be most noticed by any visitor were filled by leather-bound books of magic and alchemy. But the books on the highest and lowest shelves, and in the corners, where no one bothered to look, were cheaper, bound in cloth, or even unbound and showing their naked bundles of pages. Many of these books were romances, as Master Jenkins enjoyed a good romance, but there were books of jokes too, and of travellers' tales and wonders: *The Woman of Hastings Who Did Give Birth to a Calf and a Hare*, and *The Surprising Ghost That Hath Lately Amazed the Inhabitants of Gittings Lane with Its Melodious Musics and Most Sweet Odours*. Such stories amused Master Jenkins, as he knew – who better? – that there wasn't a word of truth in them.

Master Jenkins put down his candle on the table by the chair, picked up a cake, put it whole into his mouth, and went over to the bed. He drew back the curtain and reached for a wooden shelf built into the bed's head. From it he took a box. Seating himself on the bed with the box in his lap, Master Jenkins fished inside his clothes for a long chain, on the end of which was a key. Still chewing on his cake, he fitted the key into the lock and opened the box. Inside was a small heap of coins and jewels, and to them Master Jenkins added the three jewels he had found on the floor. All of the gems in the box had fallen from the Czar's robes. The Czar slept in his bejewelled clothes, and every bad dream tore loose a jewel. Wherever he went about the palace, jewels fell from the broken threads. They were gathered up by his servants, who returned some of them to the workshops where the Czar's robes were made. Master Jenkins kept all of those he found.

When he had replaced the box on the shelf above his pillow, Master Jenkins took another cake, picked up his candle and left his room again, passing through his small storeroom, and down the dark stairs into his workroom.

He walked the length of the dark room, shining the candle into every corner. At the end, he opened the door that the Czar had passed through and stood there a while, listening, and looking down at the dark yard, making doubly sure that no soldiers or spies had been left behind. When he was satisfied that he was alone, he closed the door and paced up the room again, into the chalk circle, where he blew out all the candles except the one he carried. The darkness came down from the roof, where it had hung in the corners; it crowded in from the corners of the room. In all the darkness of the long, high chamber, only Master Jenkins's bald head, chubby bearded face and wide shoulders were goldenly lit by the candle he held.

He walked over to the wall, shielding the candle with his hand, so that all its light fell to one side. The candle-light fell against the wooden panelling and lit up one little patch, which moved as Master Jenkins moved, walking along the wall. When he was near where he thought the door must be, he tapped on the wood. 'Christy – Christy – you can come out now.'

There was a bang as the hidden door was shoved open, and Christian almost fell from inside the cupboard. Staggering back against the wall, he tugged off the demon head and emerged, flushed, with wide, glittering eyes, to find the big room hardly less dark than his cupboard. Master Jenkins shone the candlelight in his face.

'You did well, very good, my duck.' Master Jenkins threw his heavy arm around Christian's shoulders, despite Christian's flinch. 'Even I believed you were a demon, and the Czar thought you were Lucifer himself!' He hugged Christian to his chest, though Christian was as stiff as a log with fear and suspicion. It was often Master Jenkins's joke to hug or praise and then clout. But Master Jenkins said, 'Hurry on upstairs now, and get out of that suit before anyone comes, and you shall have a cake.' So it seemed he was genuinely pleased.

Christian warmed with pleasure and bounded for the stairs, his springy tail bouncing. Master Jenkins aimed a kick at it, but jovially. 'Aye, a cake,' he called after Christian, as he more slowly climbed the stairs behind him. 'And I shall read you a story.'

Christian danced through the storeroom, a large smile on his face. It took little to make Christian happy for a while. Release from the hidey-hole, his master in a good mood, the promise of a cake and a story – that was all that was needed.

In Master Jenkins's room, Christian stood still while his master unfastened the velvet suit, and then he wrenched it off, and hid it, with its head, under his master's bed. He was naked under it, it fitted so tight.

While Christian quickly put on his clothes, Master Jenkins seated himself in the armchair with a little sigh, putting his feet on the footstool and folding his hands comfortably over his belly. He had done a good day's work, and had earned this evening of peace.

Christian, who knew what his master expected, took

the silver pot from the top of the samovar and poured a little strong tea into a glass, before filling the glass with hot water from the samovar itself. He set the glass on the table beside Master Jenkins, and moved the plate of cakes closer to him. He did not have to change his master's shoes for slippers, since Master Jenkins had never taken his slippers off.

'Would you like a pillow behind you, Master?'

'No, no . . .'

'Do you want me to go to the kitchens – '

'Later perhaps, later,' Master Jenkins said. 'You may take a cake.'

'Thank you, Master.' Christian took a cake, looked quickly at Master Jenkins and saw that he had taken up the book from the table and was leafing through it. So Christian took another cake, which he hid in his hand. He sat down cross-legged on the floor.

Master Jenkins, wriggling in his chair to find the most comfortable position, turned to the place marked in his book. It was the tale of 'The Handsome Cabin Boy', who was really a girl disguised in her brother's clothes, and searching the wide seas over for her lost lover, captured by pirates. It was the kind of story Master Jenkins loved, and he enjoyed reading aloud, giving the girl a piping but steady and brave voice, rough voices to the good seamen, and snarling, menacing voices to the pirates. Christian nibbled at his cakes to make them last longer, and listened. He enjoyed the story too, and especially welcomed it because Master Jenkins always enjoyed his own performances. The more he read, the better the mood he was in. He would probably let

Christian have another cake, and that would be three.

The story of the handsome cabin boy was near its end, but not finished, when there was a knock at the outer door, the storeroom door. Master Jenkins stopped reading and looked over the edge of the book at Christian.

Christian swallowed a sigh – which would have annoyed his master – got to his feet, went through into the storeroom and opened the door. Outside, on the narrow, dark landing, stood the two northern lords.

'Come in, my lords, go through – my master will see you,' Christian said. He spoke their language much more fluently than did Master Jenkins.

He stood aside for them. As they passed through the storeroom, the older lord looked straight ahead, but the younger looked about him at the books, and the jars and bundles of herbs.

Master Jenkins rose from his chair to greet them, clasping their hands and exclaiming how glad he was they had come to honour his little room. While he did all that, Christian dragged in two heavy chairs from the storeroom. The older of the two lords took Master Jenkins's comfortable armchair, and his son and Master Jenkins sat on the less comfortable chairs, after Christian had dusted them off.

'You must have drink,' Master Jenkins said. 'Christian!'

But Christian had already brought wine, and glasses, and more cakes, from the little cupboard at the foot of Master Jenkins's bed.

'A versatile servant,' said the older lord, with a smile.

'And a most interesting experience for us all today. I have never before seen a demon raised.' He spoke in good English, for the people of those northern cities near the borders of the Czar's lands saw more of foreigners than did the rest of the Czar's people.

'Thank you, my lord,' said Master Jenkins.

'No, I must thank your demon for speaking in our favour.' The lord smiled and, for a second, his eyes glanced towards Christian, who stood near in case he was needed. 'But perhaps the demon was – a little – direct?'

'"Grant the wishes of the men from the North",' said the younger lord. 'Blunt, Jyenkinz, blunt.'

'Isn't that what you wanted the demon to tell the Czar?' asked Master Jenkins.

'Indeed,' the older lord agreed, 'but we thought you would be more subtle. We fear, Jyenkinz, that your demon's forthrightness will make the Czar suspicious. He will suspect that we have paid for your demon's help, and then he will never grant us permission to trade with the West.'

'He never will, in any case,' said the young lord.

'My lords,' said Master Jenkins, folding his hands over his belly again, 'one thing life has taught me – subtlety is a waste of time. If I had been subtle, now, in dealing with the Czar, what would have happened? Either he would not have understood me at all, or he would have mistaken what I meant, or he would have thought, here is a man being crafty and clever – what trick is he trying? But my demon speaks to him in plain words that there is no misunderstanding or mistaking, and if he is suspicious, he thinks, would anyone who was trying to trick me be so obvious? Of course not! I tell you, my lords, if you are going to lie, make it a big lie, make it a thumping big lie there is no missing! It makes no difference in the end, because those who believe lies will believe it, however obvious, and those who don't believe lies won't, however clever and subtle you are about it. But we saw today, didn't we, my lords, what happens to those who don't believe lies?'

'Poor Pavel,' said the older lord, and then smiled at Christian, who did not dare to smile back. 'Your demon, Master Jyenkinz, might tell the Czar, in its plain way, that if he allows us to trade openly with the West, there would be much profit for him too. Such vast forests we have in the North! And there are France and England about to go to war again, and in need of timber to build ships.'

'And Germany and Holland,' said the younger lord. 'They need timber for their merchant fleets. And there is great trade in furs,' he went on excitedly. 'Beavers ruin our trees, but they make beavers into hats in Europe – we can sell as many beavers as we trap!'

'And slaves too,' said the older lord.

'Slaves?' Master Jenkins asked.

'The Lapps, you know. They are even more troublesome than the beaver. They plague our hunters and hold up the felling of the trees. It seems best to clear the land of them. Then the trees can be cut more quickly and cheaply.'

His son said, 'We should kill all the Lapps, just kill them.'

His father looked at him fondly and smiled at Master Jenkins. 'We shall kill many of them, naturally. But why kill them when we can sell them for profit, eh, Jyenkinz?'

Master Jenkins laughed, and signalled to Christian to pour more wine into the lords' glasses. Christian quickly did as he was told, stooping to pour the wine and lowering his head into the din of the men's laughter. A servant is not permitted to laugh at his betters' jokes, but Christian felt no wish to laugh anyway. He was not sure exactly what a Lapp was, but if they could be sold as slaves, then he thought they must be people of some kind, and there was nothing to laugh at in that. Christian himself was a slave of a sort, since his father – a man he could remember only as a large shape – had sold him to Master Jenkins for six pounds a long time ago, when he had been much smaller than he was now. He could not remember much of his early days with Master Jenkins, but he could remember being frightened, bewildered and unhappy.

When the laugh was finished, Master Jenkins placed his thick, chubby hands together, as if in prayer, and touched them to the end of his red nose. 'Ah – my lords – have you given any further thought to my price for this work?'

The older lord too steepled his hands. 'It may be possible to meet it. I have a cousin – a young girl, a very small estate – but connected to my family. If you are instrumental in gaining the Czar's permission for us to trade with the West, she shall be your wife.'

Christian watched as Master Jenkins lowered his

63

steepled hands to his belly and leaned back in his chair with an expression of greater satisfaction than any that Christian had ever seen on his face. 'My lord,' he said, 'my demon and I are at your service. I promise you, the Czar will give you the answer you want.'

The lords drank another glass of wine, and then they said goodnight. Master Jenkins went to the door with them, and lit them down the steep stairs himself. When he returned to his little room, he seized hold of Christian and pulled him about in a kind of rough and clumsy dance. 'I shall be a lord!' he cried. 'I shall be a lord and live in a great house, with slaves to work my fields, and a lady for my wife – and I was born a grocer's son!' And, being a little drunk, he squeezed Christian tightly in his arms and gave him a kiss on the forehead.

Christian pushed himself out of his master's grip, and then helped the old man to his armchair. 'Isn't it dangerous, Master? The Czar – '

'Dangerous?' cried Master Jenkins. He seized Christian's thin cheeks in a pinch, and said, as he shook the boy's head, 'You've never dived for pearls, Christy! It's dreadful dark down at the bottom of the sea where the pearls are – a dreadful, crushing weight of water. The divers drown, a dreadful death – and sharks eat them alive. But men still dive for pearls, Christy, men still dive for pearls!' He let go of Christian's cheeks, and slapped one of them instead. The blow was a playful one, but it stung, and made Christian's eyes water. Seeing this, his master wondered if the stock of Black Madonna's tears was running low.

'Do you want to go to bed now, Master?'

'In a moment, boy, in a moment.'

'Master?' Christian said, crouching beside the armchair.

'What?'

'Master, when you're a lord – what will I be?'

The question took Master Jenkins by surprise. He was a man who planned things, so he had most likely given some thought to what he would do with his demon when he had become a lord and had no more need of demons. But he was plainly surprised, and annoyed, that Christian had thought of it. He looked at Christian and, for just a second, there was an expression in his face that Christian did not like at all. Then he said, 'We'll think of some place for you, my duck, we'll think of some place for you.' He laughed, and flicked his fingers at Christian's nose. 'We'll send you to Hell, perhaps, eh, little devil?' And when Christian looked scared, he gave him a cake, and said he was only joking.

Master Jenkins then sat and talked happily, for some two and a half hours, of how fine life would be when he was a lord, and of all the cleverest tricks he had played in the past. And then he insisted on reading the end of the story of 'The Handsome Cabin Boy', and read it very well, though, by this time, Christian was falling asleep. But he had to stay awake to help Master Jenkins get undressed, and see him tucked up in bed, with his chamber-pot nearby. Then, when he had put out the candles, Christian was able to go to his own bed, on the floor under the table in the storeroom. He was so tired that he went to sleep in a couple of minutes.

Master Jenkins dozed comfortably for a while. But

then, in the darkness behind his closed eyes, there appeared a vivid picture of the Czar: a perfect picture. There was the long, greasy hair; the large nose; the shadowed hollows for eyes. And the expression on the Czar's face said: I know you lie to me. I know that you have always lied to me. I am waiting to see how big a lie you dare to tell me, and just how big a fool you dare to think me. And then my executioners will –

Master Jenkins bounced upright in bed, in the dark, and turned cold to the centre of his bones.

Master Jenkins was like a man who has ridden on the back of a tiger for so long – and the tiger has been so gentle and meek for so long – that the man has fallen into the habit of thinking himself for ever safe. But now and again – and usually in the night – he remembers with a horrible shock that it is a *tiger* he is riding; and he is forced to consider what will happen if the tiger ever tires of the game.

Oh God, thought Master Jenkins, his bones freezing, one day I'm going to make a mistake – or that idiot Christian will make a mistake – that the Czar can't ignore. Oh God, what if some cleverer magician with better tricks comes along and denounces me? Oh God . . .

In his mind, Master Jenkins saw the view from the scaffold – the thousands of faces upturned to watch his death. He saw the executioner pushing the tongs further into the fire – and such was the force of these unwelcome visions that his whole body was shaken by a shudder. He closed his eyes; but closing his eyes couldn't hide these pictures from him.

Hunched in his bed, his clenched fists pressed to his face, he thought, What I should do is get together all my money, all the jewels I've collected from the Czar's robes, all my most valuable books, and I should run away, get out of the Czar's reach. Maybe I should even leave Christian behind, though I have him so well trained.

For a while he sat planning his escape. But he was tired and he was drunk. For the moment he was safe. He could always run away the next night. And so, after some hours of wakefulness, he lay down and went to sleep, and when he woke in the morning, the tiger once more seemed tame, and he was again contented. There didn't seem, in the morning, to be any need to run away. How would he ever become a lord if he did?

Here, then (says the cat), is the Czar who sends hunters and woodcutters into the Northlands. And here is Master Jenkins, who knows full well that there is no such thing as magic, and that all who claim to be magicians are tricksters.

And here is Christian, who has been taught that all magic is false, and that a big lie is more believed than the truth.

And to them (says the cat) is coming Shingebiss, who is a true witch and half a shaman; and who can smell a lie. And next I shall tell more of Shingebiss.

3

Round the tree goes the cat, treading down the fallen leaves with her hard, round little feet, and winding up the golden chain.

Now (says the cat) I leave the Czar's wooden, smoky city to crouch in its own darkness beneath the dark sky.

Now I shall tell, instead, of the young witch, the lass, Shingebiss.

Through the black and silver trees, over the white snow, went Shingebiss, pushing herself with her bow and sliding on her skis, forty miles in a day.

When she needed food, she sang a ptarmigan to her, sang it right to her hand, and swiftly wrung its neck. Or, like a fox, she sniffed out lemmings sleeping beneath the snow.

When she needed to sleep, she dug a deep bear-den in the snow, and turned herself to a bear – a skinny, young bear, but still the owner of a thick fur coat – and slept without trouble. Nothing bothers even a sleeping bear, except men, and a bear that is a witch and half a shaman has little to fear from men.

It was while sleeping under the snow that she dreamed she was in the little hut again, and that there was knocking at the door. She didn't answer, and soon there was rapping at the shutters, a tramping all about the house and a thumping on the walls. A shutter flew open, and there was the face of her old grandmother peering in, calling her name, beckoning to her and shaking her head. But, in the dream, Shingebiss rose and closed the shutter again, and when the rapping and the knocking began once more, Shingebiss put her fingers in her ears and wouldn't listen. You are out in the cold, Grandmother. Stay out there, and don't bother me.

And the dream drifted into a long darkness, and into a waking, and Shingebiss shook off her bear's shape, ate some dried fish and reindeer fat from her bag, broke out of her den and went on her way.

The wind had dropped and it was a silent land she skimmed over, but with her shaman's training she heard every sound there was: the hiss of her skis on the snow, the whining of the wind in the trees and the sharp knock of one branch against another, the sudden scream of a fox.

She moved always towards the south, which she knew from the stars. Once, when the stars were covered, she asked the way of a blue fox, calling out, 'Elder sister – which way to the city, the Czar's city in the South?'

The fox jogged away, but then stopped short and looked back over her shoulder. She had taken Shingebiss to be a young bear, and bears in winter are always hungry. They will eat foxes if they can catch them. But, at a second look, the fox saw that Shingebiss was human, and took her for a boy. Boys kill foxes and make caps of their fur. Still, the bow the boy held was unstrung, and all foxes are curious. It is the way of boys to call out to foxes – men are always jabbering – but not many men are *understood* by foxes. So the fox flickered her tail and called back, 'It's good to meet a man who knows that men are the little brothers of the world!'

Shingebiss pushed back her hood to hear, and fox's ears seemed to sprout from her head to catch the fox's yap. She grinned, and then her whole head seemed to turn into a fox's head. She called out, 'Men are weak in the paw, weak in the jaw, weak in the eye, weak in the ear, weak in the nose, weak in the leg – and weak in the head! But the Czar's city, elder sister?'

'That way, that way,' said the fox. 'Opposite to the way I go!' And she scurried off over the frozen surface of the snow, holding her tail high.

But I should make this story a long one (says the cat) if I told of every mile of Shingebiss's journey, every frozen river crossed, every village skirted, every meal caught and eaten. Enough to say that nothing worth the telling happened until she reached the Czar's city, far to the south of the wild Northlands, but still deep in snow, still creaking in the grip of Frost.

She was travelling, as she had travelled for days, over frozen snow and through pine and birch trees, when she heard the sound of sleigh-bells chingling and jingling together. She smelt the rich, round stink of horse shit. Heard the clop of horses' hooves striking hard-packed and frozen snow, and the drag and scrape of sleighs' runners, smelt the tang of metal. The slithering and scuffing of many feet, the whiff of wet leather. The shouting, chattering, panting, laughing of scores of voices, and the aroma of breath from warm innards that are digesting porridge and cheese and milk. The thumping and slipping and shifting of loads in wagons and loads on backs; the earth smell of turnips and carrots, the dank smell of stored vegetables, the musty smell of dried fish. It all came through the trees to Shingebiss, and, following the smells and the sounds, she came on the road leading to the city.

The many people on the road, trudging through the twilight, made a solid dark snake, splotched with yellow from the lanterns held in their hands or swinging from the arch of sleighs. New people were always joining them, but even so the thin figure who came out of the darkness on skis made those nearest turn their heads and nudge their neighbours. Like the fox, they took Shingebiss for a boy, and, looking at her embroidered, reindeer-hide clothes, and her bow and quiver of arrows, they decided that she was a young Lappish hunter, far from home. Few of them had ever seen such a person before, but they had heard tales of them, and there were soon those who claimed to know the whole story.

'He's a Lappish prince,' they said, and the story spread, up and down the road. 'A prince of snow and reindeer. And he's cursed because he killed a bear who was his grandfather in a former life – you know all these Lapps are witches and believe the strangest things – and to make atonement he's come on a pilgrimage to our Black Madonna in the city. Only if he can take some of Her tears back to his people will the curse be lifted.'

Even those who didn't believe it thought it a wonderful story, and looked at the slender lad with something of affection. They passed him little presents of black bread and cheese, and onions and pork fat. Shingebiss, from her pack, offered them lemmings she had sniffed out the day before, and salted reindeer fat. The people laughed and thanked her, but refused.

Ahead was the city, its walls and towers a greater darkness in the snow-lit twilight. The smoke from the many fires that burned in the city, both indoors and out, rose and gathered in the air over it; and the light from the city's many fires struck upwards and lit the underside of the smoke cloud, so the Czar's city seemed to have a threatening thundercloud hanging above it always.

Little by little, hour by hour, the people shuffled along the icy road, nearer and nearer to the city gates. As they came closer yet, the sound of the many feet and iron-shod hooves, the slash of sleighs' runners through the snow – all this sound came echoing back from the city's high walls instead of fading and dying in the vast cold width of the land. And, from inside the city, to Shingebiss's ear and nose, came new sounds and new smells: hammers dancing and clanging in the foundries; a huge stink of shit and burning rubbish; a squalling of market cries; smells of cooking twining through the greater stink; a ringing of church bells. And, at last, she could see, ahead, the narrow opening of the gate.

The journey along the road was so slow because, as each person and each sleigh or wagon reached the gate, they were stopped by the city guards, tall men wearing fur caps and long, heavy, padded black coats that half hid their boots. At their sides they wore swords; in their hands they held pikes. As the people reached them, the guards held out a sack and said, 'Garnish!' And everyone threw or dropped something into the sack – something which clanked or clinked when it struck whatever the sack already held.

'What is this "garnish"?' Shingebiss asked of the people around her.

'Money,' said a shivering girl in front of her, turning a wind-chapped face with a bright red nose. 'If you don't give the guards money, they won't let you in.'

'And don't we pay enough in taxes already?' grumbled an old man behind, his bearded chin almost resting on Shingebiss's shoulder. 'But no – the Czar robs us, so his men want their share. Every time we go in, every time we come out. Robbers!' he said loudly, and then ducked behind Shingebiss as one of the guards looked towards him.

'What does your money look like?' Shingebiss asked.

The old man pulled off his thick glove, which was much dirtied by work, and showed her the copper coin lying ready on his hard palm.

Shingebiss picked up the coin, looked at both its sides, and gave it back to the old man. She stooped and picked up a pinch of the hardened snow from the roadside. Holding it in her mittened hand, she began to hum, and to sing words which the old man couldn't catch, and couldn't have understood even if his hearing had been better. But, as the old man watched, the lump of snow flattened, and changed colour, and became an image of his own coin. The old man gaped around him in amazement, to see if others had seen what he had seen.

'Lord, I wish I could do that,' he said. He peered under the edge of Shingebiss's hood to see her face. 'I've heard tell all you Lapps are witches. Are you a witch, son?'

Shingebiss smiled, and nodded.

The old man looked again at the snow-coin in Shingebiss's hand, and thought about asking the lad to fill his pockets with such coins – but he didn't dare. Lapps were strange people, whose ways he didn't know. It would be easy to offend the lad, and witches were risky people to offend. 'Good luck to you, son. It does me good to see somebody cheat these dogs' bones.'

At the gate, when Shingebiss dropped her coin into the guards' sack, it clinked just like a real one, even though it would soon be snow again. The old man shook his head in admiration.

'To the Great Square,' said the guard as he motioned them through the gate. 'Everybody to the Great Square.'

They passed through the lowering tunnel of the gate, into a crowded street, where the people all pressed forward in a pack. 'The Great Square,' people were saying all about them. 'Why are we going to the Great Square?'

Everyone in the crowd had to struggle to stay upright on the packed, frozen snow beneath their feet, and Shingebiss was swayed and shoved from behind, the side and before. She felt someone tightly clutch her arm, and looked round to see the old man from the gate.

'It will be a medal the Czar is awarding,' he panted. 'Or an announcement – more taxes! As if we don't pay enough already. Poll taxes and window taxes and floor taxes and taxes on firewood, taxes on salt – ' Shingebiss had to bend her arm and make her muscles tight to support the old man as he slithered and muttered, and clung more and more tightly to her arm and shoulder.

Winter twilight filled the streets, and the dark wooden walls packed the crowd together as they struggled forward. Guards surfaced here and there in the river of people, and the blades of their pikes caught what light there was and flashed coldly as the guards coughed, and shouted, 'To the Great Square!' and everyone struggled forward again.

Closely shuttered windows let gleams of light escape into the darkness. Lanterns hung, swinging, from lines across the streets, throwing dancing, spangling lights. People on every side: noisy, shoving people. And stink: a great stink, of sour old rubbish and choking cesspits, despite the cold. That was the city: darkness and spangled light, noise and crush and stink. Shingebiss looked up to where, above, far above and free of house-roofs, she could see the black sky with its hanging weight of silver stars.

The crowd moved into broader streets, where the wooden walls they passed were carved and even gilded, and the strings of lanterns had coloured glass in them, and threw dancing red, green and deep blue light over the dark walls and snow. There was more room here, and the people walked more quickly. The old man still clung to Shingebiss's arm, afraid of slipping on the icy snow.

Then the broad streets opened into the Great Square and there was, for yards, space for everyone to walk freely. But ahead, at the centre of the square, the people were clustering into a tight pack again, and black-coated guards were ordering all newcomers to join the edges of the crowd.

'Ever seen the Czar?' the old man asked Shingebiss. 'You want to see him. Get to the front, lad. You're young and strong. Shove to the front.'

So Shingebiss, who did indeed want to see the Czar, pushed into the crowd. Gripping her bow tightly, she would edge one arm, and then her shoulder, between people, and force them apart. Again and again she did this, squirming through the people, turning aside if one obstinately refused to move aside for her, swimming in the crowd and their warm fug of sweat, and porridge, and scented oil. Her nose was often pressed into the smell, bent against some wide back, while her hair was caught and torn out on buttons, and her feet tripped against legs. But the crowd was so dense that she couldn't fall. The old man clung to her other arm and shoulder, wriggling through the opening Shingebiss had made before the crowd closed again. He did what little he could to ease their way by shouting, 'Way! Way for the Czar!' which made people look round and laugh.

After a long time, and much effort, they reached the front. There was a space of cobbles kept clear by guards holding pikes, and then the wooden platform from which the Czar was to speak. Lanterns hung from poles at its four corners, and its stage was almost as high as Shingebiss's head, but by craning her neck and peering round the guards, she could see a large chair on the far side of the platform. The chair was draped in a material that shimmered in the light of the lanterns, and seemed sometimes black, like blood long dried, and sometimes scarlet. A brazier stood at either side of the chair. Shingebiss could smell the hot metal, and the ashes, and the coals, which smelt of long-dead leaves burning.

At the centre of the platform, in front of the chair, was a thick wooden post with chains hanging from it.

The crowd behind them swayed and threw them forwards, and the guards took their pikes cross-wise in their hands and pressed the long staffs against the crowd, and pushed them back. From behind them came cries and moans, as people were crushed in this swing and sway.

Then trumpets sounded and on to the platform, with a crashing of feet on the wooden boards, came a procession, led by four guards armed with flashing pikes.

Behind the guards came a tall, stiff figure in black fur. The old man punched Shingebiss with excitement and yelled, 'The Czar! The Czar!' The crowd shoved against their backs again, a hard, determined push which lifted Shingebiss from her feet – and the guards again set their pikestaffs across the chests of the crowd's first line and shoved them back. Some people in the crowd sank to the ground and were trodden down. There was no helping them.

On the platform, two guards came to the front, stamped their feet with a wooden boom, thumped down their pikestaffs with a wooden crash and yelled, 'The Czar!'

'The Czar!' the crowd yelled back, waving their fists and cheering and bawling, shaking the ice-crystals in the air, shaking the air, until the inside of Shingebiss's head was as dizzy and ringing with the crowd's din as her body was wrenched and bruised by their shoving.

The Czar strode to the centre of the platform and raised his arms to the crowd. His heavy fur cloak, an impenetrable black in the cold twilight, hung heavily, fluidly, to his feet. On his head, making him seem even taller than he was, the Czar wore a crown ringed with more black fur and surmounted by a golden cross. In all the crowd, only Shingebiss truly felt the pain and death that had gone into the making of that cloak and crown. And, to Shingebiss, the tall, stiff figure seemed like an immense puppet. 'Is it a man?' she asked.

'A man?' the old man yelled, and thumped her again. 'A god! God on Earth, him!'

Shingebiss lifted up her head and sniffed, tasting the air with her nose, trying to discover how the smell of a god differed from the smell of a man – but she could find no difference.

On the platform behind the Czar were more guards, and courtiers, dressed in thick furs. Leading them was a small, fat man in a new coat of fox skins trimmed with beaver, and a warm fox-fur hat. He smiled broadly at the cheering of the crowd, as if the huzzas were for him.

The Czar held out his arms to this little man, who

leaped across the space between them and hastily, clumsily, got himself down on his knees.

'That's the English wizard,' said someone in the crowd. 'I know, because I have business in the palace, me. I've seen him before. The English wizard, that is.'

The English wizard was lying on his belly on the wooden platform, at the Czar's feet. The Czar touched him on the shoulder with one booted foot, giving him permission to rise. A guard had to help the wizard up, and great gusts of steam came from the old man's mouth.

The Czar spread his arms wide, took the wizard by the shoulders – before all that huge crowd – and kissed him on each cheek. Trumpets were sounded, and cheering was raised again, each person in the crowd shouting their throats raw, because the Czar wished them to, and they knew that there were spies in the crowd set to watch them and arrest people who didn't cheer, or who weren't thought to have cheered long or loud enough.

Shingebiss watched all this as well as she could while the crowd behind her were dashing her forward into the guards' pikestaffs, and the guards were shoving her back. She thought it strange.

The Czar strode over to the chair and seated himself, and the English wizard joined the other courtiers grouped behind the Czar's chair. Still the cheering went on, because everyone was afraid to be the first to stop.

But then another procession came on to the platform, and the Czar himself held up his hand as a signal for quiet. The cheering ended at once as the people thankfully spared their throats.

The new procession was led by more black-clothed guards. The first two carried between them, in gloved hands, a brazier full of red coals, which glowed, pale and brilliant, in the darkness. Half buried in the coals were tools, of which only the handles could be seen, and even the handles smoked with heat.

The old man twisted towards Shingebiss and yelled, 'An execution! It's going to be an execution!'

And there began a crackling in the air – not the crackling of frost forming, but the crackle of many hundreds of people all realizing, at the same time, that they are going to see a killing: a crackle of excitement and fear; of loathing and eagerness. The stink of sweat that hung in the air around the crowd changed its note, became a blunter, more clubbing smell in Shingebiss's nose: a loathsome smell of fear and hunger. It tainted the air like the stink of bad meat, and made Shingebiss's skin prickle.

Now a man was led on to the platform, a man all but naked, despite the freezing cold. Against the black coats of his guards he seemed as glaring white as snow, but a second look showed how his skin had been scraped red and blue by the wind, even his scalp, for he had been shaved bald, and his beard had been shaved too. The guards led him to the post at the centre of the platform, and chained him there by the wrists, his arms above his head. His chains jangled and clattered as he shuddered in the cold. The prisoner (says the cat) was Lord Pavel.

'Ha!' said the old man. 'The cold won't worry him for long!'

A guard moved to the brazier and pulled one of the tools from the coals, which shifted and flamed. The guard brandished the tool in the air: a pair of long pincers, which glowed a rich red and made the air around them quiver. They steamed and crackled in the cold, and the crowd shifted, and sighed, and held their breath.

The guard thrust the pincers back into the centre of the fire, rattling the coals, and pulled out another pair, which glowed more yellow than red. The prisoner suddenly seemed taller as he drew himself up and stiffened. His chains chinked once, and were silent.

'Ha! Them pincers'll soon warm him up!' said the old man, and laughed – but there was fear in his voice too, and he choked.

A second guard set a bellows to the brazier to blow the fire to greater heat.

Looking at the prisoner, Shingebiss yelled, 'What has he done?'

The old man didn't know, but another man, who was being pushed against them by the crowd, leaned his face between them and shouted, 'He called Master Jyenkinz a liar – said he couldn't call up demons. Said it was all done by hidden strings and folk dressed up. He said that Master Jyenkinz had made a fool of the Czar!'

'Said he'd fooled *the Czar*?' repeated the old man, in disbelief and astonishment. 'Treachery!'

'That's the charge,' shouted the other man, swaying backwards and forwards with the push of the crowd.

'Deserves everything he gets,' said the old man, and, looking around to make sure that people heard and saw him, he shook his fist at the prisoner and yelled, 'Traitor! Dirty traitor!'

The guard once more took a pair of pincers from the fire. Now they glowed white and blue with intense heat. The guard opened and closed them, and took a step towards the prisoner, who tried to move away, but couldn't. The whole crowd fell silent with a single whoop of indrawn and held breath. The bad stink of fearful excitement thickened in the air, the worst of all the city's stinks.

Shingebiss dropped her bow, ducked beneath the pikes of the guard in front of her, squirmed between the thick bodies of two other guards, and threw herself on to the cobbles between the crowd and the platform. It was a girl who threw herself forward, but a bear whose front paws struck the cobbles. The stink of fear all around her helped her to make the change. The guards, spinning to seize the girl – or boy – who had passed them, saw a dark shape – which couldn't be a bear – leaping on to the platform. Bewildered, they stared and did nothing.

The bear made one bound across the platform, reared up and swiped at the guard who held the white-hot pincers. Backwards and over went the guard, the pincers flying from his hand. They landed on the platform and burned deep into the wood, with smoke and a stink of burning.

Then, and only then, did voices begin to cry out in the crowd. 'A bear! A bear!'

The crowd assembled on the platform shifted and swayed. Courtiers were already pushing their way down the platform steps. The Czar started up from his chair, fearing, as he always did, attack. Even his guards started back and bunched together. It was only a youngling bear, but a young bear is still stronger than a man, with teeth and nails that bite deep.

Three guards did jump forward, their pikes ready to stab – but the bear vanished. It dwindled before their eyes and was swept upwards. The guards stumbled to a halt and spun on their heels, staring about them. From above, into their faces, came dashing a soft feathered weight – soft feathers, but with claws that tore and made them drop their pikes and huddle to their knees.

A high-pitched squeal of wonder rose from the crowd, who saw a gyrfalcon, white in the lantern-lit dark, sweeping up and sweeping round, to stoop again and again on the guards. Up and around and down, the beautiful falcon, swooping now at the guards around the Czar, and now at the guards around the platform's edge – which made the crowd shriek and cower. Always, before any could strike at it, the bird rushed high into the air again and, as it poised high above the platform, it screeched – icy sound of rage – *Keeee-ya! Keeee-ya!*

A contingent of guards had hurriedly formed up and was escorting the Czar from the platform and back to the safety of his palace. All the courtiers, and all the other guards, orders or no orders, ran away with them. Seeing even soldiers run, the crowd began to break too, scurrying and slipping across the square.

Down, down, down, gyred the gyrfalcon – but when it was a few feet above the platform, Shingebiss dropped from the air with an upward flourish of grey wings. She landed crouching on the planks with a light thump, then sprang up and ran to the prisoner, who was still chained, naked and shuddering, to the post.

Pavel stared at the lad – it seemed a lad – who had been a falcon, who had been a bear, who had chased away his executioners. He could think of nothing to do but stare, and nothing to say.

Shingebiss lifted a chain in her mittened hand, gripped it, and said, 'Open! The fist opens, the seed opens, the egg opens, the womb opens: open!' In a shower of sound, the locks opened, the chains fell to pieces, and all fell with thuds and jangles to the planking. Pavel took one step from among the broken chains, and then sank to the planks, wrapping his stiff, cold arms around his cold body.

A few figures, black against the snow, were still running across the Great Square, growing small in the distance. No one was near the platform. Shingebiss went to the Czar's chair and tugged the scarlet cloth from it. There rose from it the stink of the Czar, every note of his stink, and she breathed it in, remembering it. The cloth she threw around Pavel, wrapping it about him in double and triple thickness. Pavel clutched at it, trying to be warm. He raised his bald head, his scalp and face scratched where he'd been shaved. No longer was he cocksure, or even handsome.

'Am I dead?' he said.

Crouching beside him, Shingebiss shook her head.

She rose and began pulling him to his feet. 'Come to the fires and warm yourself.'

Pavel allowed himself to be pulled to his feet and helped, as he stumbled in the long scarlet cloth, to the nearest brazier. Glowing pincers were still stuck in its coals, and he studied them as he huddled over the heat.

'When you are warm,' Shingebiss said, 'you must get away from here.'

'Where can I go?'

'To your people.'

Pavel shook his bald head, which was mottled blue and red with cold.

'Then – away from the city, far away,' Shingebiss said.

Pavel sat down beside the brazier and hugged the cloth tightly around himself, hooded it over his head. 'I am a traitor. I said what I should never have said. I called God on Earth a fool.'

Shingebiss stooped over him. 'The soldiers will come back.'

'Where could I go?' he asked. 'I have no clothes, I have no money. If I go to my home, then I make my family traitors. If I go from here naked and penniless, then any I speak to become traitors. That is the Czar's law. Anyone who gives me a word or a piece of bread or an old coat becomes a traitor. You, brother,' he said, looking up at Shingebiss, 'you are a traitor. Where should I go, brother? To whom should I speak? Whom should I ask to give me food and clothes? Whom should I make a traitor?'

For all Shingebiss's witch training, she had no answer

to these questions. She stood beside Pavel without any words to say. Then she began looking about the square, to see if their enemies were returning.

Pavel shrugged off the folds of scarlet cloth and climbed stiffly to his feet, naked as before. He shuddered as the icy air closed about his body. His hands and feet were already white with cold. 'The Czar has ordered my death, and he will have it . . .'

While Shingebiss still looked towards the palace, Pavel picked up a fallen pike. His hands were so frozen that his fingers were as stiff as the pikestaff, and he had to hold it between hands as inflexible as wooden blocks. He dragged the pike to the edge of the platform and leaned it there, driving its end into the snow heaped about the platform's legs. Shingebiss, turning, saw him throw himself down on the long, sharp point of the pike. It tore through him, and blood leaped to the hardened snow. Pavel's breath left him in a long, broken sigh, and blood spilt and spilt on to the snow, running over the smooth, frozen surface and freezing to red ice. The pike, overbalanced by his weight, fell, and Pavel fell with it, his body crashing to the ground.

Shingebiss ran to the platform's edge and jumped, landing in the snow in a deep crouch. 'Why do this?' she cried.

Pavel lay on his back, choking. She knelt beside him, and saw his eyes glazing and losing the sight of this world. There was, she knew, nothing, nothing at all she could do to keep him alive. His spirit was leaving its spirit-house. All she could do was to guide his spirit, and set it on the road to the Ghost World.

At the centre of the wide, icy, empty square, beneath the leaning weight of the black and silver sky, she sat cross-legged in the red stain of Pavel's frozen blood, and closed her eyes. She listened to the sound of the wind, coming from far, far off, and tearing itself on the corners of the executioners' platform. 'Are you cold, are you cold, my children?' She listened to the silence at the centre of the wind's whispering, and fell into that deep silence. The eyes of her spirit opened, and saw the wide road that led away from the square into darkness. She saw Pavel on the road, wandering, turning, lost and seeing nothing he knew.

She called. 'Friend . . . Friend . . .' He turned towards her voice, and she ran to him and took his hand.

There are as many roads to the Ghost World as there are people to travel there, and she led him by the shortest open to him. 'Where are we?' he whispered, and, 'Where are we going?' To have answered would only have frightened and confused him, so she kept silent and pulled on his hand, pulling him further along the road.

They came to the Ghost World Gate, which rises out of darkness and emptiness, and is hinged on the same void. Gathered before the Gate were the rustling, sighing spirits of those who dared not enter, and could not go back. Shingebiss led Pavel through them by the hand, in case their weeping should make him afraid too. But she was afraid herself as they neared the Gate. Its top, so tall, was lost in darkness. It opened only for the dead; and only shamans could open it. Only shamans could return through it. She was neither dead nor shaman; and she felt the power of the Gate pushing her away.

'Go forward,' she said. 'The Gate will open for you.'

But he hung back.

'I cannot take you further,' she said, 'Go forward, always go forward. When the Gate closes behind you, go forward. Don't be afraid.'

She pushed him, and he went forward. The Gate opened, and he went inside. He did not look back as the Gate closed. But the wind from the slamming Gate picked up Shingebiss as if she had been a dead leaf, and blew her back into her spirit-house, her body.

She saw the black sky and the silver stars above her; and felt that she had been sleeping for days and nights. But when she roused herself and sat up on the red and white snow, she found that she had not had time to be cold, and the square was still empty. Pavel's body lay beside her, the pike through it.

She rose, and found her bow, checked her quiver and threw away an arrow that had been broken by the press of the crowd. Now she would find the Czar. She started across the emptiness of the Great Square towards the palace, her bow on her shoulder and her quiver of arrows rustling at her side.

Behind her, Pavel's body lay in the empty, frozen square, fixed to the snow by his own frozen blood.

His spirit was lost in Iron Wood, and remembered nothing.

So much for him. He was a traitor. He spoke the truth. Remember (says the cat): in this world you must be mounted on a fast horse, and spurred, before it's safe to speak the truth.

4

Into the palace goes Shingebiss (says the cat) with her bow in her hand, and her arrows rustling at her side.

The cat's eyes glow, its fur bristles.

Pavel is dead (says the cat) and she is going to find the Czar.

There were guards at the gates of the palace, though they clustered together and peered out at the Great Square as if they feared attack. Shingebiss began to sing to them as she came near. 'White hare on white snow, you see me not, you see me not. White fox on white snow, you see me not, see me not, see me not. One flake of snow lost in the drift, see me not, see me not.'

The guards looked at her with open eyes as she walked up to them and among them, and yet somehow they mistook the whites of her eyes and teeth for snow, the black of her hair for the black cobbles where snow had been scraped away, and the flash of brass rings on her coat as the flash of their own pike-blades. They did start and look about as the arrows rustled in her quiver, but she added to her song: 'A bird's cheep in the city's din is heard not, heard not.' And her voice, the scrape of her quiver against her coat and the brushing together of her arrows' fletchings as she stepped lightly around and between them was heard as the rattle of a cough in a phlegmy throat, the crunch of a boot on snow – sounds heard all day and forgotten as soon as heard. So Shingebiss passed into the first yard of the palace, which was empty because the frightening rumours running about the city had made everyone hide. Some thought the execution of Pavel had been prevented by an uprising, others that it was a miracle and the end of the world was near. Shingebiss took a turn about the yard, sniffing for the Czar's scent, and finally dropped to all fours as a bear, because a bear's nose is as good as a bloodhound's. The guards at the gate took no more notice of her as a bear than they had as a girl – but a maid coming into the yard from another direction saw the bear plain enough, and ran away.

The bear entered in at a palace door, following the Czar's trail, crossed a wide marble hall, its claws clicking on the stone, and loped up a wide staircase. At the top the bear reared on its hind legs and became Shingebiss once more. A bear's nose is useful for finding a scent, but a girl's hand is more useful for opening doors, and a girl's mouth more useful for singing spells.

She opened doors and went into rooms from which other doors led into other rooms. Some were dark and cold, others were warm, smoky and bright with candles, glittering with mirrors and gilding. Shingebiss hardly glanced about her – she was following the Czar's scent.

There was a room where several men sat around a table. They were all bearded and dressed in long dark robes, with hats or hoods on their heads, and the candles threw their bulging shadows across the table and up the walls. Each man had a ledger open in front of him, and an inkstand and pens. 'White hare on white snow is seen not, seen not,' Shingebiss said as she entered, and all the men looked up – they looked down again, as if they'd seen nothing but the candlelight flickering over the panels of the door. 'A bird's cheep in the city's din is heard not, heard not.'

A boy's voice said, 'But, Masters, I've been sent to find out the news.' At the end of the table stood a boy who tightly gripped the back of one man's chair and pleaded with them all. 'Tell me something I can tell Master Jenkins.'

'The Czar is holding court,' said an old man at the table's head. 'We must keep the records. We're busy, can't you see? Go away!'

'But I must have something to tell my master, Masters.'

Another old man raised his head. 'Tell the Englishman that every prisoner in the Czar's hold has been sentenced to summary execution, and the guards are about it now. God save the Czar!'

'God save the Czar!' said everyone else around the table, and bent their heads over the books.

'I'll tell him that, Master. Thank you, Masters!' said the boy and left the room by a door behind him.

Shingebiss went round the table, following the whiff of the Czar, which she could detect among the smells of old men and candles and ink. She left the room by a door opposite the one the boy had taken, and followed the Czar's smell along a dark corridor and through another door – where she saw before her a blaze of candlelight and, black against it, the back of a large chair.

The stink of the Czar was strong there – and there was a strong smell of many other frightened people, and more ink, and food, and burning incense ... Shingebiss paused, and sang again the spell that would guard her from being seen or heard, and then she went forward, and stepped from behind the chair.

She found herself standing beside the Czar-chair, at the top of a steep flight of steps, and looking down on the courtroom. The rising draught from hundreds of burning candles touched her face with a cool warmth, and brought with it all those smells.

The courtroom was a vast, vaulted place of dusk and gold. Thick pillars curved into the low roof, making a billowing ceiling of curves. Gilded lamps hung from the curves, glittering with their own light, half obscured by their own smoke, which spilt from them and coiled in clouds among the pillars.

The great crowded chamber was filled with people, their pale faces raised towards the Czar-chair. A lamp, swinging in the draughts of air its own burning created, would light a face brightly, bring out the colour of the ribbons in the head-dress, light up the bright colours on the walls or pillar behind – and then the colours would fade as the lamp swung away. It was a place of deep, shifting shadows and sudden intense pools of light; a place of rich, vivid colours and gold; and of quenched colours – cobweb greys, indigos and darkness.

And so many people down there, in the body of the court, their faces turned up towards Shingebiss. People drawn from the whole population of the palace: black-clothed soldiers and black-clothed priests; nobles in intricately patterned brocades of every colour; maid-servants and page-boys, blacksmiths and cooks and stable-boys and kennel-boys and all. Nor was the chamber crowded with living people alone: on every wall, on every pillar and even on the curved ceiling were painted rows of tall saints who wore shimmering golden circles about their heads and gilded patterning on their robes. Staring, glowering saints who filled the little space that could not be filled by solid people.

And wafting up from the gathered people, carried by the warm, rising air of the lamps, such noise, such smells! A susurration, a deep-noted whining, groaning whispering, filled every alcove and was thrown back from the many corners and slopes made by the arched pillars – the noise made by so many, many people all keeping silent. And Shingebiss, with her shaman's training, sniffed out the many different tangs and notes of sweat, some fresh and sharp, some old and soaked into well-worn clothes. Feet shuffled against the stone floor, cloth and leather rubbed against each other; leather belts creaked and jewellery chinked and flashed sparks of light into eyes. The strong smell of the per-fumed oil burning in the lamps made Shingebiss's head ache, and she could smell the meat that the nobles had eaten, the whiff of weak beer the poorer folk had drunk with their porridge. How could they bear such a caco-phony of noise and stink day in and day out?

At the bottom of the steps on which she stood was an open space, kept clear by guards, and in this space stood prisoners, in chains. Near them, on stools, were black-clothed clerks, writing in books and reading in books. The lawyers were on their feet and dressed in grey – all of them talking and puffing out the scent of what they'd eaten.

Shingebiss turned her head to see what it was they were all staring at: the Czar-chair beside her, and the Czar seated in it. She walked down one or two steps, so that she too could look up at the chair and see it as it was meant to be seen, from below. All those hundreds of people in the hall looked straight through her: for them she melted into the smoke and candle-glare and shadows. They saw her no more than a white fox is seen against snow.

The Czar-chair had a high, wide back, shaped like a peacock's spread tail and covered with eyes of blue, green, silver and gold enamel, glittering like frost in the swinging lamplight, glittering with diamonds, emeralds and sapphires. In the chair sat the Czar, wearing his long gem-stitched robes of silk and gold, and his crown of gold and sable. Shingebiss climbed the steps again, to look closely into his face. The Czar smelt strongly, of many days' sweat, of fear and anger. His hair and beard hung in coiled, greasy strands, and his face was tight, squeezed into an expression of exhaustion and fear.

'Death!' said the Czar as Shingebiss stooped over him, and he blew a thin stream of sour breath into her face. She straightened and stepped back. From below came a jangling of chains and, looking down, she saw prisoners being hurried away by guards, and more prisoners being hustled forwards. Shingebiss sat down at the top of the flight of steps, and leaned her back on one of the Czar-chair's arms (which were carved like peacocks, and gilded).

Down below, a grey-gowned lawyer stood and shouted out, 'Mighty Czar, do not punish me but give me permission to speak!' Without waiting for an answer, he went on to state his client's case. He spoke hurriedly and in a high, breathless voice, so it might have been thought he was on trial himself. Some of the clerks wrote down everything he said, while others thumbed through their thick books, or set one book aside and picked up another.

'My client, being a man of good character, wishes to bring a case against his neighbour – the prisoner – for stealing his land. The prisoner, Great Czar, moved the boundary posts between his land and my client's, and so stole a strip of my client's land some three feet wide and a mile long. My client seeks compensation for his losses, Mighty Czar.'

The Czar spoke, above and behind Shingebiss. 'Guilty?'

Another lawyer rose and put his head close to the prisoner's. They whispered together. The lawyer raised his head and said, 'Great Czar, do not punish me but give me permission to speak. Great Czar, of your goodness, my client the prisoner pleads guilty. He was tempted, Great Czar, and fell. He knows he did wrong, he repents, he will make compensation in full, to whatever sum Your Holiness decrees, Great Czar. And he casts himself on your mercy.' Both lawyer and client went to their knees, and then to their bellies.

'Execute the prisoner,' said the Czar. 'Let the whole of his lands pass to the man he robbed. Let his crime be cried wherever his parts are hung, so that others who plan such thefts may learn from his mistake. Case closed.'

The prisoner was led away, and the lawyers said nothing at all, though the prisoner had a family who needed his land, and his neighbour had no wish to take his life or all his land from him. The lawyers knew that it was dangerous to argue with the Czar.

But Shingebiss twisted round and knelt beside the Czar-chair. She said, 'A bird's cheep in the city's din is heard not, heard not; but a whisper in a sleeping ear is heard, is heard ... Change your mind, let him live; change your mind, let him live – '

The Czar shook his head as if his ears itched, and he grimaced irritably. He called out, 'Wait!' And the guards, with the prisoner, stopped.

'Let him live, let him live, let him live,' Shingebiss whispered. When she had been learning her art, it had been a game to wander invisibly in market-places and make those selling change their prices, and those buying change their minds.

But the Czar heard voices in his head every moment: the voices of his own ever-changing moods. Often they angered him; often, having changed his mind to obey them, he would change it again, to thwart them – as now. 'Execute him!' he shouted, as if the guards were hesitating on their own account. 'And his eldest son –

let him be whipped to remind him of his father's sins!'

The constant susurration of sound from the people crammed into the courtroom faded a little as everyone there strove not to show, by voice or expression or movement, how much they disliked this order. Shingebiss was startled. She had never known anyone disobey her when she whispered orders in their ears. She looked down at the prisoner being hurried away and opened her mouth to speak another spell – but her first attempt had made things worse. She closed her mouth again.

The next case called was that of a rich merchant who wished to prosecute his old maidservant for stealing food from his pantry. He had suspected her of stealing for many weeks, and had laid a trap and caught her in the act. He had witnesses; there was no doubt. He wished her to be whipped in public for her crime . . . But the merchant looked as unhappy to be standing before the Czar as the chained maidservant. He had never expected his case, petty as it was, to be tried by the Czar himself.

The woman had no money to pay a lawyer to plead her case, and her story would have been unheard if Shingebiss had not whispered in the Czar's ear, 'Why did the woman steal?'

The Czar leaned forward, casting his long shadow down the steps, and asked, 'Why did she steal?'

The woman muttered and could not be heard. A clerk hastily stepped to her side, listened to what she said as she looked wildly about, and called, 'Great Czar, do not punish me but give me permission to speak. She says she was starving, Great Czar; that she worked all day and was fed only bowls of thin soup and one slice of bread. She says, begging your mercy, Great Czar, that many people will swear to that if asked.' And he, and the woman, and the merchant and his lawyer – all prostrated themselves.

'Mercy, Great Czar,' said Shingebiss, in the Czar's ear.

But the Czar grimaced again and twisted his shoulders under his gold and silk gown. He said, 'She is guilty, she stole. Stealing from your master, that is betrayal – betrayal is treason. The sentence for treason is death. Take her away, execute her. She'll steal no more.'

Shingebiss grasped the Czar's arm, and the Czar started at the touch and turned towards her – but though he looked into Shingebiss's face from a distance of inches, he could not see her, and did not know that he heard her. 'The moon, Great Czar, the sea-ruling moon, changes. The lion, Great Czar, the feared lion, draws in its claws. Only change, Great Czar, is everlasting. Change, Czar, change.'

The Czar's lips drew back from his teeth, his eyes squinted. He seemed to be in pain. And he cried out, 'Wait!' Again the soldiers jostled to a halt, the maidservant with them, and looked back. 'Wait!' said the Czar. 'I am merciful. I shall let her live. Burn the hand that stole. But her master!' cried the Czar, shaking off Shingebiss's invisible hand and rising to his feet. 'He who caused the crime and came snivelling here!' The Czar stooped and peered down, and his shadow

99

loomed over walls and curved ceiling. 'Knock out his teeth. Let him live on soup and find out what hunger is. And he must wear the teeth around his neck as a warning to others who would starve their servants.'

The Czar sat. The merchant was led away to have his teeth knocked out and strung on a necklace.

Shingebiss sat down against the arm of the Czar-chair and remembered her shaman's words. A mind like a broken mirror, reflecting many things and all of them crookedly.

Into the court, with a tramp of feet and a clatter of chains, the soldiers brought the family of Lord Pavel. His mother and father, his grandparents, his brothers and sisters, his wife and baby, his nephews and nieces, his cousins, his aunts and uncles, his servants, all were hustled in. A lawyer jumped up and, after begging the Czar's permission to speak, accused them all of treachery.

'Guilty!' said the Czar.

Shingebiss rose to her knees and said, 'No! They have done less than Pavel!'

But the Czar's head, just then, was filled with too many voices, of rage and terror, guilt and horror, mercy and pity, to pay any attention to one more whisper in his skull. He jumped to his feet and paced before his Czar-chair. His shadow crept and lunged over the painted walls and curved ceiling as he pointed down at the family and shouted, 'Traitors! You bred that traitor, you raised him! You hid him in the midst of my court while he planned my death! It was you, you, who set him free today! Traitors! You shall every one of you die, down to the last baby, the last unborn brat of your getting! You shall breed no more traitors to work against me!'

The Czar had forgotten that Pavel had done nothing more than call Master Jenkins a fraud. He only knew that the execution he had ordered had been stopped. Why, or how, he couldn't tell, but he feared that his people had risen against him. The Czar was like a boy who hurts and torments his dog, knowing all the time that he is doing wrong and deserves to be bitten, fearing all the time that the dog will bite him. But when the dog at last does, how angry he is; how hurt and indignant!

The Czar had always known and feared that his people would bite if he continued to torment them. Now, it seemed to him, they had, and nothing could have made him more viciously angry. He had only been protecting them from their own wickedness by ridding them of the traitors who rose continually from among them. The ungrateful, to turn on him after all his years of love and care!

Shingebiss stood too, and looked down on the prisoners: men, women, children and babies so small they had to be carried. Her eyes filled with tears, and her throat was squeezed painfully tight by sorrow. What was she to do? Her attempts to bind the Czar with spells had made matters worse as well as better. She could prevent the executions, as she had prevented Pavel's – but she hadn't saved Pavel. Nor had Pavel saved his family by killing himself. If Shingebiss saved them, would not the Czar order the arrest and execution of more and still more people? She despaired, not only of saving these people, but of saving the Northlands.

She went to the Czar's side and whispered, 'Let the whole city see their deaths – keep them in prison until the next holiday, and let it be a public execution.' She repeated this over and over, even climbing on to the seat of the Czar-chair to get nearer to the Czar's ear. She had to jump over the arm quickly when the Czar sighed and seated himself.

'Take the traitors to my prisons,' he said. 'Send my criers round the city. They are to be executed on St Nicholas's Day.'

But still the court went on, with every case, no matter how petty, being brought before the Czar for his judgement, and with harsh sentences passed, no matter how Shingebiss tried to interfere. Sometimes her words seemed to turn the Czar's anger aside, but as often as not they irritated the Czar like flea-bites and made him jump to some sentence as bad as, or worse than, the one he had already given.

The court went on for the rest of that day, and into the night, and through the next day too. In the body of the court, people lay down on the floor and went to sleep; or they left the hall and went to their beds, and newcomers came in. At the bottom of the Czar-chair steps, clerks fell asleep over their books and fell off their stools, to be replaced by others. The steps were soon black and grey with sleeping clerks and lawyers. Snores were added to the many sounds.

The Czar didn't sleep, though he was white-faced

and red-eyed. Still fiercely awake, he would spring from his chair to shout about traitors. Nor did Shingebiss sleep, though she was almost too tired to lift her head to whisper in the Czar's ear. Indeed, she was so tired that she couldn't keep her spells in good order, and many people thought they saw, from time to time, a lad sitting at the top of the steps, beside the Czar-chair. But then he would melt out of sight again, and they put it down to their own weariness and the clouds of smoke drifting through the candlelight, because of course it was ridiculous – no one was allowed to sit beside the Czar.

Then, quite suddenly, the Czar snatched up a loaf and a flask from amongst the food that had been brought to him, rose, and vanished behind his Czar-chair. A captain of the guard struck his pikestaff on the floor and bellowed that the court was dismissed. His voice echoed among the pillars and arches of the chamber. Servants turned out the lamps and blew out the candles, and the saints painted on the walls seemed to take a step backwards into the gloom, the gold of their haloes doused.

Shingebiss, with her bow and arrows, followed close behind the Czar, almost treading on the train of his robe. He led Shingebiss along wide corridors and up wide staircases. The guards at the foot of the steps would clap a hand to their eyes when they saw the Czar coming, so they could not see which way he went. Shingebiss studied them curiously as she passed. None of the guards lowered their hands or even peered through their fingers until they were sure the Czar had gone.

Through double doors and down narrow corridors, Shingebiss hurried after the Czar. They walked through darkness and lingering smoke, passing stand after stand of snuffed candles. Into rooms by one door and out by another, into the same room by yet another door and out again, up staircases so narrow that the Czar's body blocked out all the light of the lantern he carried and Shingebiss could hear the Czar's robes rubbing on the walls. The Czar made his way to bed by twisting ways, to lose – he thought – anyone who might be following him.

In a narrow, dusty and dark corridor, the Czar stopped at a door. He took a key from the pocket on his belt and unlocked it. As the Czar paused, the door still open, to check that no one was near, Shingebiss quickly slipped into the room.

There was another door opposite the first. The Czar would never sleep in a room with only one door. It was a bare room, furnished only with a couch and a stove. The floor was of bare planking, the walls of bare plaster. As the Czar closed the door, his lantern spun whirling light and shadows over the walls and ceiling.

Wearily, the Czar lowered himself on to the couch, and set his lantern on the floor beside him. Its light splayed out sideways from its glass case, and the top of its case threw a dark splotch on the ceiling. Shingebiss seated herself on the floor near the Czar, cross-legged. The lantern was not fooled by her spell, and threw her shadow on the ceiling to join the Czar's – but the Czar didn't notice that he seemed to have two shadows.

The Czar hunched his body over his knees. He stared

at the bare wall with eyes darkened by broken veins, and began to rock backwards and forwards. Steadily, to the rhythm of his rocking, he scratched his nails down his face, leaving long dark marks that would have been red in daylight. Again and again he scratched, until blood began to seep through the scratched skin. If ever he stopped scratching his face, then he began to bite his lips, which were already pitted with small wounds.

Shingebiss watched. She had meant to kill him with one arrow, and rid the world of him. But here, where he thought no one could see him, he wept, and punished himself, and groaned aloud.

If he could feel such pain, then he could be spellbound. 'A whisper in the sleeping ear is heard, is heard,' Shingebiss said, and began to sing a lullaby.

The music rose a little, and fell much, like the rise and long fall of sea waves coming to shore, or like the wind soughing and shifting among the leafy branches of tall trees. The Czar's eyes closed. His head grew too heavy to hold upright, and he sank sideways and laid it down on the couch. Sleep rose with the rise of the song, and swallowed him.

It was the Czar's habit to sleep for an hour, or even less, and then to wake in a fright. To escape the fear, he would make another journey through the rooms, staircases and corridors of his palace to find another place where, he hoped, no one would think of looking for him, and where he could sleep for another hour.

But Shingebiss's song wove through his sleep, soothing his fears and ordering his dreams to the rhythm of the music. For the first time in his fear-filled life, the

Czar slept the night through. He slept until he had exhausted sleep.

He woke to find the bare, white walls still faintly washed with lanternlight. He sat up and blinked his bleary eyes, and worked his mouth, which was dry and filled with a bad taste. And then it seemed to him that the candle-smoke, the dim golden light and the darkness swirled together and solidified into a creature that sat cross-legged on the floor close beside him. The Czar's back thumped against the wall behind the couch as he started back, with a harsh gasp of shock. His tired, sore eyes went to the doors, which he had closed and locked, as he closed and locked the doors of any room where he slept.

But the creature sat still and neither spoke nor made any move to attack him. A bow lay beside it on the floor, but it did not reach for it. So the Czar remained equally still, staring at the apparition, and asking himself what it was.

Shingebiss's appearance out of the air, in a locked room, would have filled Master Jenkins with many doubts and fears, but he would have been certain it was all a trick. The Czar, however, knew that God and Heaven and Hell and the Devil existed, without any doubt – for wasn't he God's representative on Earth? And if Heaven with its angels, and Hell with its demons, existed, then surely ghosts did too. It was plain to the Czar that this creature was either a ghost, a demon or an angel.

His first thought was that a ghost had come to him, one of his own dead ancestors, allowed to return to this world from Heaven to warn him of some danger to himself or his Czardom . . . But the creature was not dressed in the damp grave-clothes or the armour that he would have expected . . .

The Czar snatched up his lantern from the floor – making the light and shadows jolt about the room – and held it so that the light shone full into the face of the apparition. Then the Czar was sure that the creature was not human and never had been. That unearthly face, he thought, could belong only to a goblin or some other uncanny thing.

As a favour to the Queen of England, the Czar had once allowed an English artist to paint a copy of his precious Black Madonna. The finished copy was identical to the original, line for line, colour for colour, jewel for jewel – and yet the Englishness of the English painter had seeped into his paint, and his painting was a Godless English painting, impossible to mistake for the true, beautiful Black Madonna.

And so it was with the creature that sat on the floor beside the Czar. Its face, it seemed to him, was a copy of a human face made in some other world. It was much broader across the eyes and cheeks, and much narrower below, than truly human faces were. It had the shape of a cat's face, with skin that was dark gold in the lantern-light, like the gold of old church icons hanging in the shadows.

The cat's face had a cat's eyes, but these eyes were dark, not green. They reflected the lanternlight brightly, but were themselves impenetrably black – as black as the long straight hair which hung, in thin plaits and thick loose ropes, over the creature's shoulders.

The thing had a great fullness of this black hair, which hung down to its elbows. Bone-beads were threaded into the black plaits and shone moon-white against the darkness, and for a second the lantern's light blazed with hard gold brilliance on a brass sequin which, threaded in a plait of black hair, hung against the creature's dark gold face. At the Czar's court, hair was worn long and curled, but this confusion of plaits and loose hair and beads and sequins, even a white feather, seemed to him outlandish, unearthly.

A quiver of terror ran through the Czar's belly: it was a demon come to fetch him to Hell. 'Are you – 'the Czar whispered. 'Are you – '

To calm the Czar, Shingebiss smiled.

The Czar was startled by the smile. The creature's face seemed to grow broader where it was broad and narrower where it was narrow. The tilted eyes tilted even more, and their blackness caught the light and glittered. The Czar had never seen a face laugh more, though silently, and, avidly as he studied it, he could find no trace of fear, or slyness, or malice, or anger, or evasiveness, or secrecy.

A smile lacking these qualities was so strange to the Czar as to be an entirely new expression, almost without meaning for him. And he thought to himself that, though the creature had the black hair and dark skin supposed to be found in demons, it had brought no instruments of torture with it, and no unbearable stench. And could a demon's smile be without malice?

There was only one kind of creature left, thought the

Czar, that the creature could be. An angel, armed with a bow – an archer from Michael's Heavenly Army. And, having decided that Shingebiss was an angel, the Czar believed in his own decision entirely. He was Czar, God on Earth, and could not be mistaken.

'A black angel,' he said. He knew that angels could appear without wings and disguised as men, if they wished, but he had never, in all his churches, seen an angel painted with a cat's face, black eyes, and so much black hair.

Shingebiss didn't know what an angel was, and only smiled again.

'Why have you come to me, Angel?'

'To play and sing for you,' she said. She could have said, 'To bind you with spells,' and have meant the same thing.

Pleasure spread through the Czar's body, and he relaxed, leaning against the wall behind him rather than pressing against it. God in Heaven had sent one of his angels to play and sing for God on Earth! Here was proof that he ruled with the favour of the Lord! Here was proof indeed of the wickedness of those western nations, who denied that he was God on Earth! He looked with pride at his Black Angel as it sat beside him, and then thought, with a frown, of all those white-skinned, fair-haired angels on the walls of his churches, painted by ignorant artists who had never seen an angel with their own eyes.

'Did Master Jyenkinz call you here?' he asked.

'I came. No one called me,' said the Angel.

A smile spread across the Czar's face. Master Jyenkinz might, with labour and danger, call demons up from Hell. But angels came unbidden to the Czar, merely to play and sing to him! Ah, my Master Jyenkinz, thought the Czar, what is the advice of your demons worth now?

Moving suddenly from stillness, the Czar stood and held out his hand to Shingebiss, in a gesture that was an order. Without uncrossing her legs Shingebiss pressed the outer edges of her feet to the floor and rose up straight. She put her hand into the Czar's, and the Czar gripped her fingers so tightly that they were squeezed together and she could not move them. The Czar peered into her face for a moment, as if to see if it hurt. Then he crossed to the door.

'Open it!' An angel may rank high in God's creation, but it is only a messenger when all is said and done, and a Czar is a Czar.

Shingebiss turned the key, pulled back the bolt and opened the door. Into the small, dim room poured the light and heat of the many candles burning in the corridor.

The Czar hung back. 'Is anyone outside?'

Shingebiss stepped into the corridor, with the Czar still gripping her hand. She looked right and left. 'No one.'

Cautiously the Czar emerged from the room. He too looked right and left, before turning to the left and hurrying away down the corridor, pulling Shingebiss after him by the hand. Jewels fell from the Czar's gown with tiny clicking noises that were almost lost in the soft hiss of so many burning candles.

By a twisting way – going up two flights of stairs and down one, into rooms and out of rooms, and by corridors empty of people – the Czar brought Shingebiss to a large and beautiful room, lit with lamps burning scented oil. A wide couch, like a platform, spread with carpets and cushions, was against one wall. The Czar laid himself on this couch and said, 'Now, Angel, you shall meet a wizard.'

And so Shingebiss, the witch, found that fear makes a man hard to spell, and is not easy to set aside. And that is how she entered the Czar's service as an angel.

And next (says the cat) I must tell of how the witch, who has magic in her tongue, met the wizard who knows that all magic is a lie.

5

Round and round the tree goes the cat, measuring out the story in padding paws, and leaf-falls, and linking, ringing chain.

Do you remember (asks the cat) that clever English fool, Master Richard Jenkins, the Czar's wizard? The one who dresses his servant-boy as a demon and says he has called him up from Hell? The one who, because he is a trickster himself, believes there is no true magic?

Now I shall tell more of him.

When the Czar fled from the place of execution, Master Jenkins ran with him – indeed, he was one of the first of the courtiers to push aside others, clutch up his long robes, and run. He didn't wait for Christian, and he had no idea of what he was running from. He only knew that there was something that might hurt him, and he must get away from it.

He reached his room, locked himself in, and sat hugging himself in his chair, too afraid to read or even eat. When Christian found his way home, he had to knock and shout many times before Master Jenkins would believe it was only him, and open the door.

He slammed and locked the door again as soon as

Christian was through it, and asked, 'What's hap-pening?'

'I don't know – no one knows!' Christian added as his master looked angry. 'Some think Lord Pavel's family came to rescue him, but some think it was the people of the streets . . .' Master Jenkins looked dangerously angry again, and Christian said, 'But I've heard it said that it was a bear – a bear that jumped on the plat-form – '

'A bear!' Master Jenkins seized Christian by the front of his jacket and dragged him from his feet, so Christian had to clutch at his master to keep himself from falling. 'Don't talk such nonsense, you fool – a bear! No! It's –' and now he dragged Christian in the other direction, towards the inner room, ' – it's a riot, a riot, that's what it is.'

Once through the door of his room, he pushed Chris-tian away, and Christian fell hard against the cupboard at the foot of the bed. Master Jenkins slammed and locked the door, and then paced up and down the little room, clenching his fists and saying, 'The soldiers will soon put it down. Yes, this Czar, he won't tolerate it – it'll soon all be over.'

Christian picked himself up from the floor, and sat on the cupboard. He rubbed his bruised leg, and blinked, and breathed deeply, trying not to let the tears of pain and misery run. It would be a waste, as all Master Jenkins's phials of Black Madonna's tears were full.

'But if they get into the palace . . .' Master Jenkins was saying. He had stopped pacing and hunched his shoulders over, his fists clenched under his chin. 'If they get into the palace . . .' he whispered. 'They think me a favourite of the Czar! They'll blame me for Pavel's execution!' He turned and glared at Christian, as if it was his fault. Christian got to his feet, so that he could dodge if his master came for him. 'They'll lynch me!' Master Jenkins whispered.

Christian swallowed with a gulp and shivered where he stood. He thought that his master wanted him to say something comforting, but since he felt – perhaps even hoped – that the rioting mob – if there was a rioting mob – would certainly lynch Master Jenkins if they found him, he couldn't think of anything comforting to say.

'You too!' Master Jenkins said, creeping towards him, a finger held ready to jab. 'They know you're my servant. They won't care that you hate me. They'll string you up too – or they'll take you by your arms and legs and rip you apart!'

'I don't hate you, Master!' Christian said, backing away as Master Jenkins's finger jabbed painfully, and jabbed again, against his bony chest.

'You do, I know you do, but just you remember, they won't care, when they get here, out for blood. Your blood'll do just as well as mine – ' Master Jenkins broke off, and gripped Christian tightly by the shoulders as he wondered: would the mob settle for Christian instead of him? Could he say that Christian was the trickster who had fooled the Czar? Or would it be better to stick to the story that Christian was a demon? The mob would so enjoy themselves in beating and killing a demon that perhaps they would have had enough by the time they'd finished, and would leave him alone.

114

'Maybe the soldiers have stopped the riot by now,' Christian said. He was trembling because he hated being held so close by his master.

Master Jenkins came out of his thoughts, and dropped his hands. 'Then go and find out!' Christian started for the door, and was dragged back by a handful of his collar and hair. 'And go to the kitchens and get some food. Get cakes!' Master Jenkins shoved him towards the door again, and Christian unlocked it and got himself on the other side of it as quickly as he could. As he was running down the dark stairs, he heard Master Jenkins replacing the bolts behind him.

Out in the grey darkness and cold of the palace yards, Christian shivered and kept close to the walls. He clenched his jaws to keep his teeth from chattering, so he could listen the harder for such sounds as a rioting mob might make. At each corner he stopped and poked as little of his forehead round the edge of the wall as he could and still see – and then he would take a better look with both eyes – and only then would he show the rest of himself.

A troop of soldiers came swinging past, their feet crunching in the snow, and he ran to them and asked them for news. But the kindest only waved him away, while the rest looked straight ahead as if he weren't there. And, when he went on again, he saw a bear walking in at one of the palace doors, and ran off before the bear smelt or saw him. There had been a bear at the execution, it was said, and he feared it might be a dancing bear belonging to one of the rioters – which meant the rioters might be near, though he couldn't hear any shouting.

He roamed through the palace, asking where he could for news, and learning nothing until, at last, he went to the kitchens to fetch the cakes his master had asked for. The kitchen was a long building, lit like Hell by many fires, and as hot as Hell, from the heat of the flames and the boiling pots and the bodies of the sweating workers; and even stinking like Hell, since the smell of so many foods was overpowering and unpleasant. Fat sizzled and reeked, soups bubbled and filled the air with the smell of cabbage, pots were walloped, ladles clanged, cooks swore. Christian sidled in unnoticed, and he knew there wouldn't be any welcome when he was noticed. The heat made the kitchen workers ill-tempered towards everyone at all times, but they especially resented how often Christian came scrounging cakes for his master. Sure enough, 'Here again!' cried a cook, and swung a blow at Christian's head, but Christian ducked and ran to one of the huge stone fireplaces, where he edged past the little three-legged pots of sauces which stood at the edges of the hot coals until he was inside the fireplace itself. There he was able both to warm himself and to look up the chimney at winter's darkness and the icy stars. He leaned against the fire-warmed stone, hugged himself, and wished that there were one person alive who loved him.

The kitchen workers stood at the tables which ran down the centre of the kitchen. They beat eggs with a wallowing sound, and clatteringly chopped vegetables on a wooden board. They came to the edge of the fire to collect pans of sauce, and they reached up to pull down ropes of onions and bunches of herbs. Their talk was bellowed over all the noise.

'. . . was a bear, a bear!'

'Have sense, why would a bear . . . '

'. . . was Lord Pavel's family, stands to sense.'

'. . . hear *he* made short shrift of them!'

'What do you expect? Our Czar's no kitten!'

'Pavel's dead, then, for all their trouble?'

'The troops are out.'

'God help the people, God help them!'

'God save the Czar!'

And from all parts of the kitchen: 'God save the Czar! Long live the Czar!'

Christian listened, and grew warmer, and presently edged his way out of the fireplace and moved carefully about the kitchen, keeping out of everyone's way. The long tables between the fires were loaded with food: roasted chickens and long fish; plaited loaves and dishes of cream and pastries and dripping honeycombs. On one table there was a dish of little almond cakes decorated with cherries, of which Master Jenkins was very fond. Christian picked up the plate, hid it under the wing of his cloak, and made for the nearest door.

After the heat of the kitchen, the gripping, squeezing cold made him gasp, but never mind. He could go back to the warmth of Master Jenkins's room, give him the cakes and tell him that the riot was over, the troops were out, Pavel was dead and the Czar was saved. That would make him happy. He might even let Christian have a cake – though Christian ate a couple on his way, just in case he didn't. I'm a wizard too, Christian thought, I say the magic words: the riot is over, and abracadabra! I change the world for my master and make him happy when he was afraid.

Christian's news cheered Master Jenkins considerably, and he was able to settle himself comfortably in his chair to read his books and eat his cakes, only freezing or jumping to his feet if he heard a strange noise. He was not, however, made happy enough to offer Christian any of the cakes, so Christian was glad he had stolen two. 'Everything must be well,' Master Jenkins said aloud, every hour or so. 'Nothing's happened yet, has it? And it's true, this Czar, he's no kitten, he wouldn't stand for an insurrection.' A while later he would add, 'I don't know why I'm worrying. I was perfectly safe all the time.'

Master Jenkins didn't sleep well that night, but the next day Christian was able to bring him better news: Pavel was certainly dead, and his family arrested and imprisoned. Everything was going on as normal in the palace, and there was no sign of any mob, or of there ever having been a mob. Master Jenkins was still too afraid to leave his rooms, but he was easier in his mind as he sat by his stove, ate cakes and read; and that night he slept well.

He was awakened, in his warm bed, by a pounding that he at first took to be the blood in his ears. Only when he raised his head from the pillow did he realize that it was a fist pounding at the outer door. An upraised, rough voice was shouting too. At once Master Jenkins was afraid again. His heart began to jump. The mob! The mob had come – late, but it had come! A darkness moved in the darkness near his bed, and he squeaked and fell back against his pillow.

'Master!'

It was Christian. Master Jenkins reached out in the dark, grasped Christian's arm and pulled the boy to him. 'Light a candle, light a candle . . .'

He shoved Christian away and sat up in bed, staring through the darkness towards the noise of thumping. He could hear Christian groping about in the dark, shuffling and bumping against things. For a moment the pounding stopped and a voice roared out, 'Open in the name of the Czar!'

Christian had found the candle and lit it at the stove. The flame, swaying and dancing at the top of the candle, brought the bed and its curtains, the chair and the books a little out of the shadows. It showed Master Jenkins sitting up in bed, his ruff of hair sticking out in all directions about his bald head. His chubby face was pale and flabby with fright, and his eyes were large and fixed, but narrowed with anger as he caught sight of Christian's frightened face behind the candle-flame's brightness. When he felt so frightened himself, Master Jenkins hated to see another frightened face. 'Don't stand there gawping – open the door, idiot!'

'But – ' Christian looked from his master towards the din of knocking and back to his master.

' "In the name of the Czar," he says, fool! A mob wouldn't say, "in the name of the Czar". They wouldn't knock either – except knock the door down. Go and open it! But leave the candle here!'

Christian went slowly into the dark storeroom and

stood before the shaking door. The blows struck against it were so hard and loud that he flinched and put his hands over his ears. 'Open this door!' the man outside yelled, and he could hear the sound of many feet, and of pikestaffs striking the floor, and cudgels striking the walls. Perhaps it was a mob after all?

In his bed Master Jenkins was thinking, what if it was a mob after all? Could he dress and escape by another way while Christian was at the door? But no, there was no other way out. He threw himself down in the bed and huddled the blankets over his head. Better to pretend to be sick – well, he *was* sick, he felt terrible. Soldiers or mob, maybe they would take pity on him when they saw him so sick.

'Open this door! Name of the Czar!'

Christian pulled back the bolts and turned the lock as quickly as he could: better to get it all over with than go on being afraid. He was sent staggering back as the door was shoved open.

In came a soldier, dressed all in black. He gave Christian the merest glance before seizing him by the collar and shoving and dragging him through the storeroom and into the room where Master Jenkins was hiding in the bed.

Pushing Christian aside, the soldier grabbed the covers and threw them on the floor. There, on the mattress, lay Master Jenkins in his nightshirt, hiding his head. 'The Czar summons you!' said the soldier. 'Now!'

Without raising his head or opening his eyes, Master Jenkins felt around himself with one hand, trying to find the bedclothes. He didn't know they were on the floor. 'I'm sick,' he said. 'Very sick – *mal* – *krank* – '

The soldier turned to Christian, whom he knew to speak his language better than Master Jenkins. 'Tell him the Czar orders his presence – now! No excuses, no arguments – now!'

Christian edged around the soldier and collected Master Jenkins's clothes from the cupboard, where he had folded them earlier. He took them to his master and whispered, 'Master, the Czar has ordered you to come now, straightaway.'

'I'm coming, I'm coming!' Master Jenkins cried. He sat up and began putting on his clothes over his night-shirt. Christian helped him tug on his robe, and fetched his boots. 'Dress *yourself*!' his master cried. 'You're coming too!'

But Christian was dressed – it was draughty in the storeroom. While Master Jenkins was still treading his foot into one boot, the impatient soldiers led them, by the light of lanterns, down the stairs, through the work-room and out into the freezing yards.

Across yards, into buildings, out of buildings and across other yards the soldiers led them. The yards were silent, biting cold and dark. The long corridors were chill and dim, and silent except for the quiet tramp-tramp of the soldiers' feet – but the passages became more brightly lit and warmer as they went deeper into the palace. Painted, twining green vines spread along the walls, sprouting red and golden flowers, and tall, glowering figures of saints or heroes looked out of alcoves. The soldiers stopped outside a double door studded with gilded nails and set in a carved frame. The Captain knocked with his pikestaff, and then the doors were thrown open, and Master Jenkins and Christian were shown into the private apartments of the Czar.

A vast, low room, glimmering with gilding, smelling of burning flowers from the perfumed oil in the lamps, and forested with thick pillars and arches which threw many deep shadows. The walls were painted with processions and hunts which flared into bright colours near the lamps, and faded into greys and browns in the shadows. The ceiling had many graceful curves and arches as it flowed down into the pillars, and was painted black with gilded stars, while the sides of the pillars were pictured with tall, watchful saints or fierce, armed heroes.

They could not see the Czar at first, because the pillars blocked their way. Master Jenkins bent himself double and made his way forward like that, so that he would be bowing as soon as he came within the Czar's sight. Christian quickly copied him.

They rounded a pillar on which a black-bearded, scarlet-clothed hero was throttling a snake, and saw a low dais built across one end of the room. It was piled with furs and cushions, and here the Czar waited for them, half lying and half sitting. As soon as he saw the Czar, Master Jenkins dropped to his knees and then went to his belly; and as soon as he saw his master do this, Christian did the same. No one's head was allowed to be higher than the Czar's.

But even with his forehead on the floor, Master Jenkins was straining his eyes in their sockets to peep at the Czar, trying to guess what sort of mood he was in. The Czar's hair hung on the embroidered shoulders of his robe in greasy, twisted strings; his face was pale and his eyes red. His clothes had been slept in; they were crumpled and creased. Experience of the Czar had taught Master Jenkins that these were bad signs. And yet, beside the dais, close to the Czar's hand, was a low table, covered with dishes and jugs – and in the Czar's very lap was a dish of fruit. That the Czar was eating had always been a good sign – or, at least, not a sign of the worst.

'Jyenkinz,' said the Czar, 'have you spoken with your demon since I saw you last?'

Oh God, this was the worst. Master Jenkins could not answer for the faintness that washed over him, and sickened him. Oh God, he knows, he knows: he knows I've done nothing but lie to him. He forced a wheezing breath through his throat and managed to say, 'Not – since then, Great Czar.'

Christian, a little behind his master, kept his head down and did not dare to look up. He was always afraid to look at the Czar, and now he simply hoped that the Czar had not noticed him. If he didn't look at the Czar, he thought, perhaps the Czar would not see him.

'You coil of dung, Jyenkinz,' said the Czar. 'How you studied, for so many long years, to learn to call demons from Hell. Risking your life and soul each time. Preparing yourself by starving for days – '

Christian's fear made him want to giggle at this, for he knew that Master Jenkins never, never starved. He bit his lips and held his breath to keep himself quiet.

'Afterwards, cleansing yourself of the taint of Hell. And I ' – the Czar clapped himself on the chest – 'I do none of this. Yet I am visited by angels. Because I am God on Earth.' And with a movement of his hand, the Czar directed them to look at the other end of his dais.

They swivelled their eyes in their sockets to look. There, where the Czar pointed, were no lamps, and in the shadows another figure was sitting, very still. Its head was higher than the Czar's!

It sat cross-legged on the dais, and much black, black hair hung loose and in plaits over its shoulders and down to the cushions; and the blackness was studded with moon-white beads. Its face was strange, unlike any Christian or Master Jenkins had ever seen, and certainly unlike any they had ever imagined an angel having. It was, Master Jenkins thought, a monkeyish face, better suited to a goblin than an angel.

Master Jenkins had travelled a good deal in his life, further than the Czar had ever travelled, and he had talked with people who had travelled even further. He knew that the people of different lands do not all look alike. When Master Jenkins looked into the face of the Czar's Angel, he saw someone as human as himself. Someone who was, therefore, a liar and a trickster.

Underneath all the fear that Master Jenkins felt there began to wriggle anger, and jealousy. Another trickster, come to wheedle the Czar's favour away from him. How had the impostor convinced the Czar that he was, of all things, an angel? Had there ever been anyone, what with that black hair and that monkey's face, who looked less angelic! But it was a big lie! Master Jenkins had to admire it.

What tricks did such a bold trickster know? How good was he at sleight of hand? Could he make a demon-suit half as good as the one Christian wore?

'My wizard, Angel,' said the Czar. 'He raises demons, to find for me the Elixir of Life.'

The impostor, the Black Angel, turned its head towards the Czar. 'What is that?' There was nothing angelic about its voice either, except to the Czar's ears.

Master Jenkins wanted to laugh in the impostor's face and ask how it was that an angel was ignorant of the Elixir of Life, but he did not dare, in case it annoyed the Czar.

But the Czar was frowning. 'The Elixir of Life, Angel. The secret of life eternal, the power that will give me life for ever.'

The Angel laughed, which startled everyone. Master Jenkins was astonished that the impostor dared to laugh. Christian – who thought that the creature might be an angel – was astonished that it *could* laugh. The Czar was merely astonished, as he could not remember anyone ever before daring to laugh when he had spoken seriously.

'Nothing lives for ever,' said the Angel.

'Do not punish me but give me permission to speak,' Master Jenkins gabbled. 'Surely, Great Czar and Angelic Messenger, surely the Lord lives for ever?'

'The Lord?' said the Angel.

An angel who has never heard of God! thought Master Jenkins, and peeped at the Czar but if the Czar had noticed the Angel's ignorance, he gave no sign of it. Master Jenkins could not think, at that moment, of a way of pointing it out that would not seem to accuse the Czar of being a fool.

'Shaman,' said the Angel, 'live for three hundred years, but their bodies grow old and worn, and they are glad to die at the end. They live long to learn the roads to and from the Ghost World, and the nests in the Iron Ash.' Shingebiss looked up at the Czar. 'But unless you are claimed by a shaman at your birth, and raised and trained by a shaman, there is nothing that will keep you alive for even three hundred years.'

The Czar stared back at the Angel. From his expression it might have been thought that his face had been slapped. He drew in a deep breath, and Christian turned his face away, and Master Jenkins shivered with frightened glee – but the Czar held his breath, and then let it out, and forced back the corners of his mouth in a kind of smile. The Czar wanted his Black Angel, the proof that he had the favour of God in Heaven, and an angel must always tell the truth. If an angel lies, then it is no angel. So the Czar had to accept that what the Angel said was truth, but it was easy to see that he didn't like it. The Czar's gaze began to turn towards Master Jenkins.

'Oh, Great Czar, oh, unhappy, unhappy!' Master Jenkins cried. 'Demons have lied – lied to me!'

'Demons always lie!' said the Czar. 'And you – dung! You can call only demons – and they come eagerly, ready to fool you with their lies. You cannot call angels! Angels will not come to your call!'

'Only to yours, **Great** Czar, only to yours,' Master Jenkins agreed, bowing his head to the carpet again, and with fiercer and fiercer hatred growing in him for the impostor. 'Forgive me, Czar, forgive! I will away go. I am shame, shame – I believe demon's lies!'

'Take your stink away,' the Czar said.

Master Jenkins at once began to shuffle backwards on his knees, as Christian was already doing. 'Thank you, thank you,' Master Jenkins said, as he went.

'Out of my sight!' the Czar yelled.

Master Jenkins shuffled faster, until a pillar hid them from the Czar, and then he leaned on Christian while he got to his feet. Together they hurried from the apartment.

As they made their way through dim, candle-hissing corridors and across dark, frozen yards, Christian said, 'Are we going away, Master?'

'Away?'

'Away from here, Master. To – Denmark?' Christian had an idea that Master Jenkins had bought him in Denmark, and he always hoped they might go back there.

'No, no, we shan't be going anywhere,' said Master Jenkins, as if the very idea was foolish. 'Go and get me something to eat – to settle my stomach.'

When Christian reached Master Jenkins's room, carrying the tray of bread, honey and fruit, he found Master Jenkins sitting in his chair, leaning his chin in his hand. He set the tray on his master's lap, and then made the bed, and fed the fire in the stove while Master Jenkins ate. Christian kept taking quick looks at his master, to see what kind of mood he was in, and, at

127

last, said, 'Isn't it dangerous, Master, to stay here? The Czar told us to go away.'

'Stupid! He told us to leave his room. If he had wanted us to leave the country, or even the city, he would have made that clear. No, no, Christy, the Great Czar hasn't finished with us yet!'

Christian had gone to sit on his stool, and gripped the edge of its seat with his fingers, while he tucked his feet underneath it. 'No?' he said, thinking of the heads stuck on spikes over the city gates, and the parts of bodies hung in chains at the street corners.

'Christy, you can't read people as I can!' Master Jenkins laughed to himself in excitement. 'Why do you think our fine Black Angel said there is no Elixir?'

Christian found himself unable to answer. He knew that Master Jenkins often lied, and that his magic was often mere trickery, but he thought that, still, he might know some *real* magic. And how did he know whether the Elixir of Life existed or not? Or whether the Angel was truly an angel in human shape and spoke the truth, or whether it was a human liar?

'Oh, Christy, Christy, the answer is simple. Our friend wishes to take my place as wizard to the Czar – and so he's trying to make the Czar think badly of me. "There is no Elixir," he says – but you see how cleverly I got around that, Christy? The demons lied to me! How can I help it if the demons lie to me – you naughty demon, you, Christy!'

Master Jenkins laughed again, but Christian didn't feel like laughing. It seemed to him that he was being blamed.

'Our Black Angel has been too clever for his own good. Did you see the Czar's face? The Czar wants the Elixir more than he wants anything, more even than he wants to boast of a black angel in his service. He'll soon grow tired of mercy and pity and all those other angelic things. We won't have to wait long, Christy, before we're back in favour! I think when we are, I'll ask for more money than ever before to buy ingredients, and then I'll almost discover the Elixir, but fail, and then I'll almost discover it again – and then I'll ask for more money – and *then*, I think, I'll give the Czar the Elixir.'

Christian jumped a little as he sat on his stool. 'There really is an Elixir, then?'

'I'll give him pig's blood to drink,' said Master Jenkins. 'No, he might know what that was. Red water, then, with something to make it taste foul. He won't believe in it unless it tastes foul and costs a lot.'

'But red water won't make him live for ever, Master.'

Master Jenkins looked at Christian steadily for a moment, and then kicked out at him, but couldn't reach him, and was too idle to get up and kick him properly. 'You are a stupid boy. You've learned nothing. I give him something which he thinks is the Elixir – well, so long as he's alive, he'll believe it's working, won't he? And when he dies, he won't know it isn't. And long before he dies, I shall be a lord in the North, and I shall have sold my estates and gone back to England a rich, rich man.'

And where will I be then? thought Christian.

*

129

Where indeed (asks the cat)? But Shingebiss is going to spell the Czar and change him – so all Master Jenkins's plans may come to nothing.

But first (says the cat) I must tell you more about this land, and the Czar, and his palace.

Around and around the tree goes the cat, treading down the fallen leaves, winding up its golden chain.

The Czar (says the cat) had always been afraid to sleep, ever since, as a child, the nobles of his court taught him the meanings of the words 'murder', 'assassination' and 'death'.

Sleep is the little death, and while you sleep you cannot see who is sneaking close to you, with knife or smothering pillow. Always the Czar had kept sleep away however he could. For days and nights on end the Czar would hold court, with clerks snoring in little deaths around him, but would not sleep himself. He would pray for nights and days in the chapels and churches of the palace, kneeling so long on the stone floor that he could not stand, and banging his forehead on the altar steps at the end of each prayer. The cold and the pain kept him awake.

Or he would spend days studying the science of numerology, giving each letter of his own name a different number, and adding and subtracting them according to complicated schemes. He believed that the answers to these sums – if he got them right – would reveal his destiny. If the numbers didn't promise him eternal – or, at least, long – life, he decided they were wrong and started again with another system, or with different numbers.

Or – in former times, before his Black Angel came to him – he would spend hours talking with Master Richard Jenkins about the hierarchy of Hell, the methods and dangers of calling demons, and how much reliance could be placed on their word.

Even when he was so tired that he stumbled as he walked and saw ghosts – as very tired people do – the Czar would still keep himself awake by sending for musicians, or actors. Theirs was no easy task, to perform for a silent Czar who propped up an aching head and gloweringly watched them through red, sore eyes. No music, however light and dancing, could make him tap toe or finger; no joke, however funny, could make him smile. And he cared nothing for the stories of the plays and songs, being too tired to follow them. He wanted only noise to keep him awake.

And, when sleep could no longer be kept away, when dreams traipsed before his open eyes, when his whole body ached and urged him to lie down, then the Czar would creep away, secretly, to some small room where he could lock himself in. There he would sleep a few hours before fear woke him and sent him sneaking to another room where he could sleep some more.

And so, for years, the Czar had taken little part in the ordering of his Czardom, or even of his palace. For the many days at a time while he was praying, or studying numerology, talking with Master Jenkins, listening to actors or musicians, or sleeping, the palace and the country were ordered by the Czar's advisers and officers. And a merry time they had of it.

The Czar's soldiers were slaves and were paid no wages – but they were given food for their bellies, uniforms for their bodies, boots for their feet, weapons for their killing. There were whole regiments of ghostly soldiers who didn't exist, who were no more than names written in the rolls of his armies, but for whom the Czar gathered food, and had uniforms, boots and weapons made. The Czar's officers took all these things and sold them for their own profit.

The officers in charge of the palace kitchens asked for twice the food needed to feed even the vast horde of people living in the palace, sold what was not used and pocketed the profit.

The Czar might find the rich guilty and send them to execution – but if the Czar was not in court, then no rich man or woman was ever found guilty of any crime, because they could afford to bribe the officers of the court with expensive gifts. Poorer folk, who could not afford such bribes, were always found guilty, because such property as they had was then made over to the officers of the court.

The officers in charge of collecting the taxes for the Czar demanded far more than was right from everyone, and kept the difference for themselves. They were confident of not being caught. After all, the poor could not complain unless they could afford to bribe an official to listen to them, which they could not. And those who could afford the bribes could only complain to another officer, who would say to them, 'To accuse a Czar's officer of such misdeeds is *treason.*' That silenced the complaint, since everyone knew what the punishment was for treason.

And this is only to consider the Czar's officers, who were all noblemen. Besides them, there were maids who stole and sold the fine waxen palace candles and the scented lamp-oil, and kitchen servants who stole food from the kitchens for their families. There were stable-boys who stole the horses' hay and oats and sold them. There were seamstresses and tailors who stole the cloth and the thread and the buttons and the jewels. Carpenters stole wood, blacksmiths stole iron – everyone stole what they could. Goods were carried into the palace in carts, and carried out in bags and under coats, in pockets and boots and sleeves.

It was said that if ever an honest man were to enter the palace, then the very walls would cry out in praise of him – but who had ever heard the palace walls so much as whisper?

Because of this thievery the palace needed, every year, more candles than before, more grain than before, more cloth than before – more of everything, every year. And it was the poor, all across the Czar's land, who had to provide the more and more, by working harder and paying more.

But then came the Czar's Black Angel.

No one who was a murderer, the Czar felt, would dare to approach an angel. Or, if they dared, the Angel would know of their presence. So the Czar felt safer with his Black Angel by his side, and kept Shingebiss with him always, often holding her hand to be sure she was there. As long as his Angel was with him, the Czar did not feel that he needed to force himself to stay wakeful, and though he still crept away from everyone to small rooms in distant parts of the palace, he slept more often. That alone made the Czar a little clearer in his mind.

And knowing that his Angel sat beside him, on guard, made the Czar's sleep still deeper and easier. The lullabies Shingebiss sang brought peace and sleep within moments, and the sounds that rose from her single throat made the Czar even more certain that she was not human. Deep, soft notes that made the darkness and candlelight whirl together; high, soaring notes that seemed to shoot through the golden darkness with a silver trail like shooting stars; and the sound of a flute, its sweet, hollow notes vibrating in the wooden tube with the player's breath. And yet there was no flute-player, but only Shingebiss, singing.

The gentle singing set the darkness quivering about the Czar's head, and the song's chant rose a little and fell much, like the rise and long fall of sea waves coming to the shore. The Czar felt himself sink away from wakefulness, and when he tried to rise up again – as he always did when he felt sleep overcoming him – then the song called him away and called him away, soothing him and calling him. Even after the Czar was sound asleep, the song went on with him, into his dreams.

In his lullaby-dreams the Czar walked through a forest, over snow. The trees were black against the snow, and above was a cold, black, black sky full of silver stars. A thin, freezing wind made its way through the trees with a whine and a moan, hardening the snow, polishing the stars. It touched the Czar's face with cold so cold it was a touch from a burning iron. His breath made a silver mist about his face, and froze into white ice in his beard.

Walking with him was his Black Angel, its great cloak of beaded, braided and loose black hair washing and drifting about its shoulders. The beads made clicking sounds in the cold air as they clattered together. The Angel looked at him and smiled its strange smile, but it no longer sang.

The wind, and the clacking of beads – those were the only sounds. And their own movement, and the slight movement of a branch tip here and there, were the only movements. Not a bird, not a mouse – there was nothing else living between the white snow and the black sky.

The forest vanished. All the trees had been cut down. On every side the whiteness ran away and ran away, white, barren white, to meet the black sky. On all that whiteness, nothing moved except the scouring clouds of ice-crystals and snow that the wind blew before it.

The Angel spoke to the Czar. 'Your hunters have killed the Northlands.'

The Czar, looking about him, nodded and smiled. In such a blank, white landscape, no one could creep near him without being seen. There could be no surprises. He approved of what he saw.

When the Czar woke from this happy dream of an unchanging world and emerged from his hiding place – leading his Black Angel by the hand – he sent for food and ate an enormous amount. Then he went to the bathhouse and steamed himself crimson and clean. He had his hair combed and oiled and curled with heated tongs, and he dressed himself in clean robes of embroidered and gem-sewn brocade. It was no longer his habit to go for months without washing or changing his clothes. Nor did he spend his time in praying or numerology.

It was at this time that he sent for the officers of the Imperial mint, and gave orders that new coins were to be struck. They were to be of gold, silver and copper, and they were all to show the figure of the Czar on one side and the figure of the Czar's Black Angel on the other. The Czar wished everyone in his Czardom to know how God had favoured him with an angel.

The officers prostrated themselves, and dreamed of the gold and silver they could steal while the coins were being struck.

'And I myself shall oversee the minting of these coins,' said the Czar. 'Everything is to be brought to me for my approval.'

The officers went away, still cheerfully looking forward to being richer than they were already. The Czar often threatened to inspect their work, but forgot his own threats within a few hours, and began a week of praying instead, or studied demons with Master Jenkins.

When the officers of the mint were gone, the Czar sent for his artists. He was tired, he told them, of the angels painted on the church and chapel walls of his palace. These angels had been painted by artists who had never seen an angel, and they all had blond hair, white skins, and white wings. He wished these false angels to be chipped from the walls, and replaced with paintings of his Black Angel, so that the people who prayed in his churches, in future, would know what a true angel looked like – and, of course, would remember that their Czar was so favoured by God that God had sent an angel to him without his even asking for one.

And the artists all prostrated themselves, and happily thought of the expensive colours they could order, far in excess of what they needed, and keep. Lapis lazuli, the most expensive colour of all, ground down from semi-precious stones! Malachite! Gold leaf!

'I shall oversee this work closely,' said the Czar. 'I wish to see the sketches before you begin. You may go.'

And off went the happy artists, thinking, as the officers of the mint had done, that the Czar did not mean what he said. They would prepare their sketches, bring them for their approval – and find that the Czar was no longer interested in seeing them. Then they could get on with their painting and their thieving in peace.

But soon they heard news that made them think again.

The Czar, it seemed, was looking about him for tasks to fill his time. Or was he seeking to find fault with his people, so he could punish them? He demanded to see the accounts of food withdrawn from the palace storehouses for the kitchen. He went himself to the warehouses, holding his Black Angel by the hand, and he counted the sacks and barrels that went from there to the kitchens. And then he went to the kitchens, and counted the dishes that went to the tables. And he himself examined the ledgers kept by the officers of the kitchens. The Czar's arithmetic had been sharpened by his study of numerology. He read no destiny of his own in the numbers he added and subtracted in the kitchens, but the destinies of the kitchen officers were clearly foreshadowed there. The numbers told the Czar that he was being cheated and made a fool of. The officers of the kitchens were arrested and sent to prison to await trial for treason. They were replaced by cooks and serving-men who were – for the time being – much too afraid to steal.

The Czar then turned his attention to the officers of his army, and soon there were new officers, while the old officers filled up another prison cell.

Honesty came to the palace, though the walls were still not heard to cry out in praise of anyone. The seamstresses, the carpenters, the tailors, the black-smiths – all began to practise honesty and to hope that no one would find out that they had ever done anything else.

It was too late for the officers of the mint and the artists, though the artists were allowed to finish their paintings of the Black Angel before they were sent to prison.

The Czar held court. The artists, and the officers of the mint, kitchen and army, were brought before him, and he listened calmly to all that was said, for and against the prisoners. Nor did he continue night and day, but stopped frequently to eat and sleep. But at the end, when he had heard all, he gave orders for every thief to have his right hand cut off.

The Black Angel sat visibly at the Czar's side and no longer had to whisper invisibly in his ear. 'Czar,' said the Angel, 'if you cut off an artist's hand, how is he to earn his living?'

'Honestly,' said the Czar. 'Is there any doubt that they are thieves? None. Did anyone force them to be thieves? No. What is the punishment written in the law for a thief?' He pointed to a lawyer at the foot of the Czar-chair steps.

'Great Czar, the punishment written is, for a first offence, the right hand to be cut off.'

'Then cut off the hands of these thieves.' And the Czar smiled.

'But, Czar,' Shingebiss said, 'all are thieves, but some have cheated you of fortunes, over years, and some only stole a few cakes for their families. Are all to be punished alike?'

The Czar laughed and clapped his hands together, as if he was enjoying the argument. 'Whether you steal a gold bar or a cold cake, there is but one word for you – *thief*. The hands of thieves are cut off. Their hands will be cut off. And,' he said, bending from his tall chair towards the white-faced prisoners, 'if you are caught stealing a second time, your left hands will be cut off.'

'Show a little pity, Czar,' Shingebiss said.

'Whining, always whining of pity!' said the Czar. 'Pity is for God and for angels. Pity they will find in Heaven, if they reach it. I am Czar, my kingdom is the Earth, and I punish sinners as they deserve, to guide them on the way to Paradise. Take them away,' he said to the guards. 'Chop off their hands.'

Others came before the Czar: lords who wished to send more hunters into the Northlands, to provide them with more furs; merchants who wished to send more woodcutters – 'The price of timber is rising, Czar. The city needs more.'

Unhappily Shingebiss listened as the Czar gave permission for more animals to be trapped and killed, for more trees to be cut down. She said nothing, knowing that nothing she could say would move the Czar.

Again and again, as the Czar slept, she shaped his dreams with her songs and showed him the dead land he was making; but though the Czar grew calmer under her spells, he grew colder too. He did not care. And he gave permission to more hunters, and more, to enter the Northlands, with their guns, their traps and snares.

Another lord came and said, 'Great Czar, please to examine this map of the estate which you allow me to enjoy.' And he handed a rolled map to the Captain of the Guard, who carried it up the steps and put it into the hand of the Czar.

The Czar unrolled the map, and Shingebiss looked at it over his shoulder – an angel is permitted to look over a Czar's shoulder.

'Great Czar,' said the lord, 'please to notice the lake.'

There was the lake on the map, coloured a pretty blue. The artist had drawn fishing boats on its waters, and reed beds around its edges with water birds flying from them. Little drawings of houses showed where villages were built on the lake's banks. Shingebiss, looking at the pretty map, heard the sound of the water, and the bird cries, smelt the mud.

'Great Czar,' said the lord, 'already I send many wagon-loads of food to your city, to the profit of us both. I could send much more, and make us higher profits, Czar, if my land was better watered.'

'Do you expect me,' asked the Czar, 'to come and spit on your land?'

'No, no, Great Czar,' said the lord, unsure of whether or not he should risk a laugh at the Czar's joke. He decided not. 'But if, Czar, if I had your permission, Great Czar, to dig trenches to carry the water from the lake to my fields – then crops would be turned into gold for us both, Czar.'

Shingebiss, in her quick mind, saw the water draining from the lake and the little ships grounding on the dry, cracking mud; saw the fish thrashing as they choked in the air; saw the reeds wither and the birds fly away; saw the people of the little villages starve without their fish and game, while the crops they grew were sold to the city.

'No,' she whispered in the Czar's ear. 'No.'

The Czar turned to her and said, 'Go.'

It was strange to see an angel surprised.

The coins with the figure of the Angel stamped on them had already been issued in the city. Everywhere, the Czar fancied, his people were studying the picture of the Angel and thinking of those black wings spread protectively over their God on Earth. Never would it be forgotten that God so loved the Czar Grozni that He sent him an angel to do him honour – but the Angel itself was a tiresome thing, pleading as it did for kindness and mercy. Better, after all, perhaps, to have eternal life than an angel.

'Leave me,' said the Czar. 'Come to me when I wish to sleep.'

Shingebiss rose and passed behind the Czar-chair, to the steps and the door which led from the courtroom. She could have stayed, invisibly, and whispered in the Czar's ear, unheard, as she had done before – but that had only done harm. She remembered that the old shaman had told her she would fail. A mere witch, as she was, could not hope to spell the Czar.

After she had gone, the Czar went on holding court for a little time, but soon called a halt. He sat in his chair while everyone waited, then rose and left the court-room, and the court was dismissed.

The Czar prayed in his private chapel and afterwards went to his rooms, and all the while he was thinking of angels and devils, and God and death. An angel may guard a Czar from his nightmares and his mortal enemies, but can even an angel keep death away? Only the Elixir could do that.

The Czar's splintered mind never held any one reflection for long.

He sent for his steward, and had a present sent to Master Richard Jenkins . . .

Shingebiss walked through the dim corridors of the palace, and the breeze of the many burning candles touched her face lightly with a smell of burning, and brought the faint scent of a dead forest from the wooden walls. She passed guards on duty at doors and at the foot of staircases; she passed maidservants and manservants. All went to their knees at the sight of her, because the Czar had ordered it – but some lowered their eyes and crossed themselves with such devotion that she saw they truly believed her to be an angel sent by their God.

She took a candle from a stand and, by backstairs and through empty rooms, made her way to one of the small chambers where the Czar sometimes slept. It was empty of furniture except for the Czar's couch, and Shingebiss sat in a corner, leaning her back against the painted wall. Above her head ran a painted hunt, mounted men on horses chasing deer through painted trees and patches of candlelight and shadow.

She stared into the ragged candle-flame as it shifted in the draught blowing from the door, stared into its red heart, and thought of the Northlands in summer, when the dark fir trees tipped their branches with new, golden growth, and the birch put out glowing green leaves. She saw the slender shapes of fish teeming in clear water, and looked up into a sky of a fragile, harebell blue. She watched the sky turn black and fill with winter's silver stars, and looked about at the wind-shaped snow, its soft curves and knife edges. And a pain of longing went through her for her own north country, and a spasm of sickness for this fetid, smoky city.

If a witch couldn't spell the Czar and save the North-lands, could a shaman? Perhaps there was need to be a shaman after all.

To become a shaman, a witch must take the road to

the Ghost World, pass alive through the Ghost World Gate, and enter the world of the dead and the unborn. She must travel through Iron Wood, and yet remember her own name, and find her way back, alive, to her own world.

Witches who enter the Ghost World for the first time are taken by their shamans; and even after that, when they are new-made shamans, older shamans guide them, teaching them the road, and the way through Iron Wood.

But Shingebiss's shaman was dead. Dying, she had said, 'Go to my sister in the East', but Shingebiss had not. If she was to go to the Ghost World now, she must go alone.

She stared into the candle-flame, seeing in its light the things of which she had been told – the rainbow bridge over void and chaos, the World Tree, the Iron Ash, and the Gate itself . . . She knew it was a fearful thing she meant to do.

She slipped her soul loose and went spirit-travelling.

And we (says the cat) will follow her, to the Ghost World.

7

There are many, many worlds (says the cat). They are caught and upheld in the branches of the World Tree, and we visit them in dreams, without wishing to do so or knowing that we do. But a shaman – or even a mere shaman's apprentice – who knows how to slip off the body and go spirit-travelling may visit them by choice.

Some of these worlds are so like this one – except that they are not this one – that it is said that anyone who goes wandering on the eves of Midsummer or Midwinter – those between-nights when time is not – may, in one step, pass from this world into another and, perhaps, may never know that they have left their own world, and their own fate, behind.

Others of these worlds are so different from ours – though not more strange – that no one without a shaman's training could find their way into them, much less find their way back.

And the Ghost World? It is not so strange – nor yet familiar. It is the first world, and the last – the world where the sleepers dream the beginnings, the ends, and all the histories of all the other worlds.

And into these worlds Shingebiss dived like a fish, to look, and breathe, and twist out of them and into others, as sleepers, dreaming, may slip from one dream into another as their bodies shift in sleep. One glimpse, one sound, was enough to tell her, *not here*, and send her sliding into another world.

And thinking of the Ghost World, filling her mind with all she had been told of the Ghost World, soon brought her to its Gate.

She stood among the red, smoking fires built by those who had found the Gate but dared not enter through it. The fires stank greasily, and their red light could show only a small part of the Gate as it towered into the darkness above them. The light glimmered redly on the Gate's strange hinges, which let the Gate open any way it was pushed. There was no wall to the Gate, and yet no way through.

Fear filled Shingebiss. Everyone fears to stand there, before the Gate. Even greater was the fear that the Gate would open and admit her to the Ghost World – and close for ever behind her. Her spirit-body shook with fear, and she felt the roll and pull of the blood pulsing in the body she had left behind – and with a jolt, a shock like falling, she awoke in the small room of the Czar's palace, under the painted hunt.

After the Ghost World, the Czar's palace seemed frail, as if its walls were of paper, as if the candlelight were shining through them, not on them. No sound came from the corridors and rooms beyond, and all she could smell was the burning candle and the dust. And if the Czar's world seemed like a dream to her, then that is what it was – a dream of some sleeper in the Ghost World.

Shingebiss lay down on the hard floor, wrapped her arms around herself, and shook and shook. She knew it was dangerous to enter the Ghost World while afraid. Her fear had made her spirit recoil and fly back to her body, and in its fear and confusion, it might easily have become lost in another of the many, many worlds. But Shingebiss had no shaman to take her into the Ghost World. She must put fear away, find courage and go through the Gate.

Lying in the little room, she recited to herself all the names of all the shamans who had gone before her into the Ghost World, and had returned. The long list calmed her and, as it went on, made walking into the Ghost World seem as ordinary and common as stepping out to the privy.

She sat up, and closed her eyes against the sight of the little candlelit room and its painted walls. To herself she said, 'When you poke your nose out of doors, pack courage and leave fear at home.' And she said, 'When you go living into the Ghost World, eat nothing, drink nothing, if you wish to return.' And then she tipped back her head against the wall and sang, clapping her hands softly together because she had no drum. And, again, she slipped loose of her body and went spirit-travelling.

She opened her spirit-eyes and stood before the Ghost World Gate, but now she refused to feel the fear that the sight brought. People moved around her, passing from fire to fire, and some had no faces and no shapes, because they had waited there so long, afraid to enter, that they had worn away. 'I shall be a shaman,'

Shingebiss said, and went forward to the Gate.

She leaned against it. Under her hand she felt the ridges of the wooden planks, hard and smooth as iron. She felt the roughened hinges. Leaning her cheek against it and closing even her spirit-eyes, she thought of nothing, nothing, nothing . . . Until the pull of the blood flowing in her far-away body quietened and quietened so she could not feel it. Almost, it stopped. And the Ghost World Gate swung away from her hands, swung open for her. She flung herself inside.

She fell to the ground, and grass blades of thin iron crinkled under her. Behind her, the Gate closed. At once she felt a rush of exultation at her own courage that almost stunned her, and made her, for a moment, blind and deaf to the sights and sounds of the Ghost World, which she had wondered about for so long. Her body, spirit though it was, glowed with strength and pleasure. Strength and power rushed through her and tingled in her fingertips, in her ear-tips, her nose-tip, pounded in her heart, with a heat and a strength she had never known before. Because now, now, she was a shaman. The Ghost World Gate had opened for her and had closed behind her. She had, willingly, walked so close to death that the Gate had opened for her, and she had passed through it, willingly, without fear, and had allowed it to close behind her, shutting her away from life. And still she did not fear: her excitement and new strength were too great.

She would go forward, into Iron Wood, among the dead and the unborn, knowing that she need never be afraid of anything again – and this, she understood, was why a witch becomes a shaman on passing through the Ghost World Gate. This was why a shaman was powerful. Shamans were not hampered by fear for themselves and, without fear for themselves, they had full use of all their power.

Inside the Ghost World Gate huddled more ghosts, who had had the courage to pass through the Gate, but were afraid to go on into Iron Wood. Shingebiss was so filled with her own strength and fearlessness that she hardly paused among them, but darted forward to enter the wood by the nearest path.

She passed through trees of living iron, with grooved bark that peeled in rust. When a wind blew, the leaves rattled and jangled like keys in a bunch, or rang out clearly like a cymbal, while under her feet the fallen leaves, rusting, scraped and grated. It was an autumnal forest, Iron Wood – every leaf was tinged with red.

There were others wandering the forest ways – all lost, because they trudged with down-hung heads, no longer bothering to look about them, or looked everywhere with eager, bewildered faces, hoping to see, to find – what? The happiest there – excepting the new shaman – were those who had laid themselves down and gone to sleep. They are the dreamers who dream us.

Shingebiss made her way through Iron Wood, turning this way and that through the iron trees, jumping across rusty streams, tearing herself on steel thorns. Always, in the iron trees all around her, there was singing – not birdsong, but not human song either. There were many voices, all singing as if to themselves.

It was a place that could frighten, if the wanderer there could feel fright – but Shingebiss still glowed with the knowledge of her own courage and power.

Depths of fallen iron leaves moved under her feet as she went, grating and scraping. She followed the thought of her grandmother, turning and taking a new path when she felt that she must, and so she was led to the World Tree.

The World Tree, the Iron Ash, grew at the centre of Iron Wood. Up and up grew its iron-grey, pearl-grey, moon-grey trunk, high above the other trees, high into the sky. Immensely wide spread its branches. At its foot, among its roots, was a deep pool, its water black, but tinged with red rust: the Well at the World's End. Shingebiss stood and looked down at the dark water with its slow, silver ripples. She could smell the water, smell the iron in it, and she wanted to drink, but knew she must not. Instead, she walked around the tree, a long walk. She saw a flash of red among the grey branches – the stone squirrel that ran up and down the tree. And, high, high, she saw the eagle that perched among the tree's topmost branches. But she didn't find her grandmother.

Shingebiss lifted her arms, leaped, and turned into a gyrfalcon, which flew up among the Ash's branches. It flew through the iron leaves and keys and up and up. It looked down on the Ash's iron branches, which were as broad as lands, broad enough to hold herds of deer, horses, pigs. In many places, among the twigs, were nests, but it was not birds who made their homes in these nests. They were the homes of shamans waiting to be reborn. The shamans slept, or played with feathers and bones, or took food from the spirits who attended them.

Shingebiss saw her shaman, lying curled and sleeping in her nest like a tiny, ancient baby. The gyrfalcon alighted on the nest's edge, and shifted its shape so that Shingebiss slid into the nest, among the soft old feathers, and broken shells, and fishbones. Shingebiss bumped against the shaman and woke her. Milky eyes opened in the crumpled, ancient face, and peered at the lass.

'Don't you remember me, Grandmother?'

'Oh, I remember you.'

'And you didn't wait for me – down there, by the Well? Have I been so long in coming?'

'Why should I have waited,' asked the old shaman, 'when you made no haste to come to me? Did you go to my sister in the East?'

Shingebiss looked away. 'You know I didn't, Grandmother.'

'Did you think I wouldn't know, here, in the Ghost World? I scryed for you, Shingebiss. I saw you disobey me. And have you spelled the Czar and saved the Northlands?'

'No, Grandmother.'

' "No, Grandmother." You were too clever. Go away now, and be clever.'

'Grandmother, I'm a shaman now.'

'Is that what you call yourself? You are brave, that I will grant you – but it's more than courage makes a shaman. See if your shamanry will let you find your way back to your Northlands – and then go to my sister in the East. Humble yourself to be an apprentice again, and finish your training with her. Then come here to me again, and I may call you Granddaughter. Until then, you are a stranger to me. Go away.' And the old shaman turned her back on Shingebiss, and curled herself up to sleep again.

Shingebiss sat in the nest for a while, trying to find the words that would make her grandmother forgive her and turn to her again – but all her training and her new-found shamanry could not do it. And then she was angry that all her new strength and her pride in becoming a shaman should have come to this – a snub from an old woman. She rose, stepped the edge of the nest, spread her arms and turned into the gyrfalcon.

In her bird's shape she could have flown over the Ghost World, flown over the Gate, and so returned to this world of ours. But her anger could not last, and a weight of sadness tugged at her and dragged her down to the floor of the forest. Her bird shape fell from her and the toes of her boots rustled into the iron leaves. She sat down beside the pool of rusty black water, too sad to cry. All her pride in her shamanry fell from her. She had thought she could spell the Czar, she had thought she could save the Northlands, and she had been wrong. What should she do now? Return to the world of her birth, and live on there, watching the Northlands die around her? Should she take an apprentice of her own, and teach her the three magics, while the forests were cut down, and the lakes drained, and the animals killed? Shaking her head, she rose to her feet. It would be better to lose herself in Iron Wood, a forest that could never be cut down.

So she left the Iron Ash, and pushed her way through intertwined branches that clashed their leaves like gongs, and whipped back, when she released them, with the force of a spring. Thorns and briars grew up through the branches, tangling them together with thorns like razors and spikes, scratching her skin with long, thin, painful scratches – for when shamans travel in other worlds, they go in spirit-bodies which feel pain. It was hard to push a way through the thorns, but, when she turned to go back, the branches had closed the way behind her.

A thin tunnel led through the briars, and so she ducked into it, the thorns tearing at her hair. Ahead of her, as she struggled, she heard a wolf howl, and she stopped to listen. The iron branches and leaves all around her, settling into stillness, rang and clinked and jangled.

She followed the howling of the wolves, always pushing towards the sound, no matter how the steel thorns clung together, no matter how fiercely they scratched. And the tangle of trees and briars ended, as if they had been cut down, and she came into a cleared space – a yard before a palace. The yard was guarded by wolves. They ran towards her, their black lips lifted from their white teeth, their blue and yellow eyes glowing, their thick grey fur hardened and blackened with dried blood. Shingebiss stood still and showed no fear of them, and though they sank their teeth into her clothes and tugged at her, they did her no harm. When

154

she began to move again, towards the palace, she had to push against them, and they followed her, pushing against her legs as she went.

The palace was built of splendour and decay. Its high roof was gilded and caught the dim light of the Ghost World and threw it back a dull gold, like a dying sunset. Its roof was bare, rotting laths and black holes.

The long timber walls were carved with intertwining lines and tall figures carrying wine cups, and the carvings were gilded, and glinted and gleamed . . . The walls were spoiled by damp and moss, the wood crumbling, the gilding falling from the blackened figures.

Shingebiss drew near the doors, and they were beautiful, of polished wood, set with gilded nails, decorated with shining hinges. The doors hung from broken, rusted hinges, with holes where the nails had rusted into blackened wood, with long splits where the wood had swollen and cracked.

All this Shingebiss saw clearly, with open eyes. The hall was both a palace and a ruin. Where timbers were rotten, they were also whole; where the roof gaped, it was also gilded.

She reached the door, stretched out her hand and pushed against the smooth, polished timber, the sharp, gleaming nail-heads. The door crumbled at her touch, rustling to the ground in heavy dust, its sharp smell of damp and wood rising into her face. She stepped into a hall as filled with stored cold as a stone vault. It stank like a grave.

The hall was lit by torches and fires, giving that golden light which seems bright, but which hangs over everything like a shifting golden veil, and through which you must peer to see clearly. Tapestries or rags, tapestries and rags, hung from the walls, and the hall was filled with benches, on which sat richly dressed and beautiful people. Shingebiss walked down the hall, and her feet released the scents of spices and lavender from the rushes she trod – and she looked and saw skeletons seated about her, in colourless or blackened rags. There was no scent of lavender, only the stink of decay.

But the beauty, the riches, the sweet perfumes were not illusions. Nor were the stinks, the ruin, the rot. Shingebiss knew that she had found her way to Hel's hall. All that she saw there was equally true.

Hel ruled the Ghost World, the Queen of the dead and unborn, and she gathered to her hall, to her court, all those who had been famous for their cunning, or for their singing and playing, for their poetry or their beauty – all those who were, in some way, remarkable. The rest Hel left to wander in Iron Wood.

The dead drew aside as Shingebiss made her way through them. They stared at her, they even leaned to look into her face from their own beautiful and decaying masks, but none spoke to her. The dead cannot speak unless the visitor to their world speaks to them. Musicians, singers, poets . . . but no shamans. When shamans come living to the Ghost World, they leave without calling on Hel; and when shamans come dead to the Ghost World, they find their nest in the Iron Ash, and don't seek to remind Hel of the souls their shamanry has saved from her.

156

Indeed, there is little love lost between the Ghost World's Queen and the shamans who so often trespass in her world.

The hall seemed to grow longer and wider as Shingebiss walked on, and the ranks of the silent dead seemed to grow ever more numerous, until it seemed to Shingebiss that she might walk through that hall, through its mingled scents and stinks, for ever. And so she began to clap her hands and to chant Hel's name, and that soon brought her, at a final drawing back of the dead, to the hall's high seat.

The high seat was set between wooden pillars which were both gilded and rotting. Embroidered tapestries, beautiful and mouldering, hung around and behind it. One half of the seat was empty. In the other half sat Hel, her face half beauty and half skull, dressed in a queen's robes and grave-clothes, crowned with golden corn and mould.

Shingebiss stood among the dead and looked up at the Ghost World's Queen, trying to see in her face only the colours of life, and only the smoothness of living flesh. But Hel would not be so contained by little magics and, as Shingebiss watched, all flesh withered from Hel's face and body until she sat on her throne, a stained skeleton, wrapped in grimy rags. In the silence, the hall about them darkened; the tapestries fell into rags, the timbers parted, and the graveyard stink grew thicker.

'A shaman,' said the skeleton, Hel. Her voice was soft, low and warm. 'Creeping, creeping, into my world, into my hall, to my very throne-chair. Why so

157

brave? Have you come to steal the finest of my souls from me?'

'I have come to steal nothing from you,' Shingebiss said. 'I have come to ask if you will receive me here, in your hall, and let me stay.'

'You are alive,' Hel said. 'I hear the tread of your feet in the rushes. I see the warmth of your living body hang about you. I can smell your blood. I can hear your heartbeat, a world away.'

Shingebiss sighed and sat down cross-legged on the floor of Hel's hall, among the rushes and lavender sprigs. The tall dead stared down at her.

'If I go back through the Gate,' she said, 'it will be to watch the Northlands die. Tree by tree, fox by fox, bear by bear . . . I thought I was clever and could stop it, but . . .' She shook her head.

Hel laughed. Shingebiss looked up and saw that the skull of Hel's face had taken on flesh again: withered flesh clinging to bone. 'Why did you think that you – you – could halt change?'

Shingebiss smiled. 'I was a fool. I am a fool.'

Hel rose, and held out her hand. Her finger-bones came out at the end of her fingers, as if the flesh of her hand were a worn-out glove. Shingebiss put her hand into Hel's cold one and got to her feet. She followed where Hel led. Hel's grip was like the squeeze of the arctic cold.

Swiftly, Hel led her through the crowds of silent dead, who drew back, their feet making no sound. Shingebiss was led the length of the dark hall, past hangings whose embroideries seemed to move, and then fell into rags. They passed, in darkness, through a door and Shingebiss saw, ahead in the darkness, a light that flickered and glimmered.

It burned by the side of a curtained bed, and its dim light stained the bed-curtains a dull brown. The darkness was thick around the frail light: a darkness that shifted as the lamp flared; a darkness full of silent movement, of unheard sound.

Hel, her fingers still clenched about Shingebiss's hand, turned to her and smiled. That side of her face lit by the lamp was a woman's pretty face, softly fleshed. The other side of the smile, the other eye, was hidden in darkness. 'My bed,' Hel said, 'is Sickness; its hangings are woven from Misfortune.'

Shingebiss started, and her hand tugged against Hel's grip. Her grandmother had taught her those words, when she had taught her about the Ghost World. She watched as Hel drew back the curtain. The swish of the cloth set the darkness whispering and gathering into greater blackness that dimmed the lamp.

Behind the curtains was a bed, and from the bed rose a scent of lavender, and homely, human sweat, and a faint tang of earth and decay. Someone lay in the bed, in the darkness.

'Lift the lamp, and look,' said Hel.

With her free hand, Shingebiss took up the little pottery lamp and held it so that its faint, shimmering yellow light fell into the bed-space. There she saw the rise and fall of a man's chest, the ribs showing and then sinking into flesh – white flesh, stained blue, as if bruised.

She moved the light and saw an outstretched arm,

bent at the elbow, the hand resting on the pillow, fingers loosely curled – a white hand with blue nails.

She shifted the light again, and it fell on the face of a most beautiful man – beautiful, but with the colouring of death. Flesh as colourless as snow, with dark hollows beneath the eyes, and dark lips.

Shingebiss looked at Hel, and the light of the lamp lit Hel's beauty, and touched the edges of the bone on the shadowed side of her face. 'This is Balder,' Shingebiss said. 'First to die, and first among the dead.' And she shivered where she stood, to think that she now saw, and moved among, those who had been, to her, only wonderful stories.

In the bed, Balder shifted, twisted, clenched his fist and fell back limply into his pillows.

Shingebiss stooped over him again, careful to hold the lamp so that no hot oil should spill on him. 'He dreams bad dreams.'

'He dreams,' said Hel, 'of trees cut down, of lakes drained, of the bite of traps, and of death, and death, and death linking death.' Hel tipped back her head, and spoke as if of pleasures. 'Deaths of great trees and little beetle deaths, deaths of birds; deaths of foxes, of wolves, of bears . . . And then the deer and the little voles and mice, dying of hunger . . .' Hel giggled.

Shingebiss watched a moment longer, as the sleeping man threw one arm across his closed eyes, and turned from the light.

'He dreams of the Northlands' dying.' Shingebiss set the lamp on its little shelf once more, and its light no longer fell into the bed-space.

'Were you not taught,' Hel asked, 'that your world is dreamed by the dreamers in the Ghost World?' Her hand, a fan of bones, reached into the darkness of the bed, as if she would touch the sleeper's brow. 'The little dreamers doze beneath the trees in Iron Wood, and they dream a little flower, a stream, a mushroom. They dream prettiness for a baby, they dream a kiss after a quarrel, a fright in the dark . . . But Balder is the first among the dead. His dreams – and his nightmares – shape your world.' She smiled again. 'Why don't you jump into his dream, shaman? Why don't you twist and shape his dream, and change the fate of your world?'

Shingebiss took a step back from the bed and she shook her head. She knew it was not in her power, or in the power of any shaman. Balder was of the first people, the oldest. While he had lived, there had been no death in the world.

When Loki, Balder's brother, shot the mistletoe dart into Balder's heart, the Gate of the Ghost World opened for the first time, and Balder passed through it, opening the way for others to follow. Balder's dreaming in the Ghost World began the call to follow him there; then pain, and loss, and regret came to the world. And Balder's dreams had been shaping the world now for a thousand thousand years, and longer yet. His dreams were wide and deep, and full of power, as real as the waking world, and more real, since they made it.

Shingebiss took another step from the bed. To enter Balder's dream would be to enter the very heart of the world's pain; it would be to feel every breaking loss, every regret that ever drove its pain deep . . . There

161

would be much beauty too, as the world is full of beauty: an agony of beauty. Shingebiss shuddered as she thought of trying to shape that dream. There could be no shaping it. It would shape her.

Hel still held her hand. Shingebiss twisted her fingers and clasped the hand that was clasping hers. 'Lady Hel, *you* could change it. You could wake him – you could whisper in his ear and change his nightmare to a dream!'

Hel laughed, full, loud, happy laughter, that echoed back from walls unseen in the darkness. She loosed Shingebiss's hand and, instead, put an arm around her shoulders – an arm that felt heavy and full-fleshed. She led Shingebiss from the sleeping-chamber, back to the hall crowded with the tall ranks of the silent, staring dead.

'The shaman thinks I should wake him!' she called out to the dead, who began to titter, all around them, rustling, obedient titters: rain falling on leaves. 'Let the trees fall! My forest grows thicker. What dies in your world lives in mine.'

'Not the same life,' Shingebiss said.

Hel took her arm from Shingebiss's shoulder, and seated herself again on her high seat. 'Long ago,' she said, 'when Balder died, all things in your world wept. A ransom in tears, to free Balder from my hold.' She closed her eyes. 'That was music! Never before or since has there been such music!' Her eyes closed.

'No music from Loki,' Shingebiss said, remembering the old, old stories. Loki, Balder's brother, and the first to walk the road to the Ghost World alive, the first to pass alive through the Ghost World Gate, the First Shaman. Loki, Balder's murderer, who would not weep for him, and left him in Hel's hold for ever.

'Never will there be such music again as the "Lament for Balder",' Hel said. 'But the lament for the Northlands' dying, that music will be sweet, and I must hear it.'

Shingebiss turned her back on Hel, and would have left her, but the tall dead moved, swaying, into her way, making a wall that she could not pass by. She turned round and looked at Hel, who now seemed, as Balder had done, a beautiful corpse. 'Did you not ask if you might stay in my hall?'

'I am alive,' said Shingebiss. 'I am a shaman. You cannot keep me here.'

'From your world to mine is a hard journey,' Hel said. 'Wearisome, to be a shaman: wearisome to drive yourself to trudge that long road again and again. Now you are here, in my world, where all your journeys will end, at the end . . . Why struggle to return? Why hold yourself so different from your brothers and sisters? Eat, drink, then lie down and rest, and dream . . .'

Hel's voice was soothing, and to Shingebiss her words seemed lovely. Shingebiss turned again, and found Hel's attendants holding out to her a plate and cup. A plate holding the fruits of Iron Wood, and a deep cup filled with Hel's dark brew, bitter with the tang of iron and rust. One bite of that fruit, one sip of that drink, Shingebiss knew, and there would be no return through the Ghost World Gate for her, even though she was a shaman.

And why return? She thought she saw a way to break Balder's dream, and change the fate of the Northlands, but was she more likely to succeed than she had before? And though she lived three hundred years, she had to die at last . . . Why not, indeed, drink and sleep?

She took the cup from the hand of bones that held it, and tilted it towards her, and looked down into it – and, in the dark hall, the darkness of the drink in the cup made a mirror, a black mirror, like a shaman's scrying mirror. She looked into the darkness, with thoughts in her head of her own world, and her own heart, beating a world away . . .

In the blackness of the cup, she saw pictures. In the blackness she saw red, red . . .

What (asks the cat) did Shingebiss see in the cup?

That I will tell in a while, but not for a while.

For while Shingebiss has been in the Ghost World, things have not stood still in our world, and I must tell you of the doings of the Czar, and of Master Jenkins, and even of Christian.

8

Do you remember the English wizard (asks the cat)? Do you remember his Danish servant-boy?

Do you remember the wizard's workroom, where he raises demons for the Czar? And the steep stairs that lead from the workroom to the storeroom, where the wizard keeps his grimoires, his crocodile dung, his baby's fat?

And the snug little room beyond that, the wizard's private sitting-room?

A warm little room, its shutters and its door shut tight against the winter ice, and the winter's thin, sharp draughts. A warm little room, its candles glowing against the winter dark. The blue and white of the stove tiles shone in the candle-haze, the bed-curtains hung in warm brown folds and dark shadows, and the glasses on Master Jenkins's table and the coins in his hand glinted and glimmered. There was a heavy winter smell of hot candle-grease, and warm dust, and old wine and perfume.

Short and round, Master Jenkins sat in his armchair, wrapped in a long warm robe, with his feet up on a stool. His damp face glowed a cheerful red and across his lap was set a tray, on which he was counting coins.

Occasionally he took up a grubby little notebook from his table, dipped a quill in his ink-pot, and wrote. Beside the ink-pot stood an open bottle of wine, a glass, and a dish of cakes.

Christian sat on the floor, leaning his back against the bed. The skin of one side of his face was darker than the other, and his lip was scabbed. In one hand he held a sliced onion and with the other hand he held a small glass phial to his cheek. Tears ran down his face and into the phial. At his feet was a small wooden box, in which leaned many little glass phials, some already filled and corked, others empty.

Beside Christian, on the floor, lay a bundle of long black feathers. Where the candlelight shone on them most brightly, other colours could be seen beneath the black. They were the long dyed tail-feathers of peacocks.

'How many now?' Master Jenkins asked, as he wrote in his notebook again.

Christian counted the filled phials. 'Eight, Master.'

'I need eleven! Take a good sniff of that onion – or if the onion's no good, shall I fetch you a clout? How many feathers are there?'

'Six, Master – and another four in the dye.'

'We haven't sold one in a week!' To Christian's surprise, Master Jenkins raised his red face and smiled. 'No one wants to buy the Black Angel's feathers any more! I told you it wouldn't be long before the Angel lost the Czar's interest. How could he keep it, when he was fool enough to say that the Elixir doesn't exist? You must tell people what they want to hear, Christy. No matter what tomfool rot it is – if it's what they want to hear, they'll believe it.'

There was a knock at a distant, wooden door – not at the door of their room, but of the outer room, the storeroom. Christian looked up, alarmed, into his master's face, and Master Jenkins looked at him, in as much of a fright. It was all very well to speak of winning back the Czar's favour, but a knock at the door did not always bring good news.

'Well – answer it!' Master Jenkins said.

Christian put down his phial and onion, got to his feet and opened the door. A blast of cold air blew in from the storeroom, and Master Jenkins shivered and threw his robe around his feet.

Christian picked up a candle and went out into the chill storeroom. His candle's light wheeled over the ceiling and touched brightly, briefly, against the glass jars on the shelves, lit the gold lettering and locks on the grimoires, fell flat against the door's wooden panelling and iron locks.

The knock on the door came again, making Christian jump and the candlelight leap. 'Open! In the name of the Czar!' shouted a voice from outside.

Christian turned the heavy key in the lock and tugged back the bolts. He dragged open the door, and a brighter light than his candle shone at him from the small landing outside.

Peering against the light, he saw three men, one holding up a bright lantern. They were warmly dressed in thick mittens and furs. One held a large glass bowl, which sparkled in the light, and the other a small, fat barrel. Their breath swirled like smoke in the light of the lantern.

While Christian still stood blinking, the man holding the lantern cried out, 'For Master Reechod Jyenkinz, a gift from our Ever-Ruling Czar!'

The three men stood, stiffly upright, waiting. Christian took the glass bowl – which was filled with caviare – into the crook of one arm, and clutched the little cask in the other. 'Thank you, thank you,' he said. 'Er – Master Jenkins thanks the Czar.'

The lantern-holder frowned, as if he thought better thanks should be offered than this. 'The Czar wishes that Master Reechod Jyenkinz shall attend him at noon tomorrow,' he said, and turned. The two other men turned too, in the narrow space, and they marched off down the stairs, led by the lantern-bearer, whose light soon vanished into darkness.

Christian, awkwardly clutching the bowl and the barrel, kicked the door shut, and went back through the storeroom and into the heat and light and candle-smoke of Master Jenkins's room. Kneeling, he managed to let the little barrel drop on to the floor with a thump, and then was able to set the glass bowl more carefully on the table beside his master.

'From the Czar, Master.'

Master Jenkins kicked up his feet. 'From the Czar, from the Czar! What did I tell you, Christy?'

'The Czar wishes you to attend him at noon tomorrow, Master.'

'The Czar wishes me – ! Ah, Christy, we're back in favour! Look, the best caviare! Hand me that barrel!'

Christian lifted the little cask into his master's lap, and Master Jenkins sniffed at it. *'Brandewijn!* What time tomorrow?'

'Noon, Master.'

'The Czar is hankering, Christy, hankering for what only I can give him – the Elixir of Life! And I shall give it to him, and get rid of that damned Black Angel at the same time! I shall have an estate, Christy, and be a lord! Now, toast! Toast is what we want, boy! Go and get toast!'

Christian unhooked his cloak and hat from the back of the door, wrapped himself in them, and went down the stairs and out into the freezing night, where the icy wind blared across courtyards, buffeted the ears and scraped the skin from the face. And, as he made his way through it to the kitchens, Christian wondered all the time, what would become of him when Master Jenkins was a lord?

But though Master Jenkins seemed to be so happy at the thought of being called to the Czar, his sleep was broken that night by fear-filled dreams, and the next day, as he made his way through the palace corridors, across dark, cold yards and in through doors to other corridors, he was not happy.

He came to the doors of the Czar's private rooms, where black-clothed guards stood. They stared at him without smiling – they never smiled – and Master Jenkins felt still more unhappy. The guards rapped on the doors with their knuckles, and Master Jenkins watched as the doors swung inwards, revealing a glimmering, gauzy haze of candlelight glowing on paintings of many colours. A thick perfume drifted to him, carried on the breeze of the candles.

Master Jenkins dragged his robes about him, and walked forward into the Czar's rooms, trying to pretend that his heart wasn't shaking him with its beating, and that he felt as bold as he would like the guards to believe he was.

He made his way forwards through the musky smoke and the forest of pillars, passing painted saints and heroes who glowed in robes of scarlet and lapis lazuli and held gilded shields. On rounding one of these pillars, he caught sight of the Czar and dropped to his knees, bowing his head.

The Czar was lying on his dais, propped up by cushions of many colours, with golden fringes and embroidery. Beside him, on a low table of polished green stone, was set a meal of wine, dates, bread and dried apricots. The Czar watched Master Jenkins crawling towards him over the rugs.

Coming nearer still, Master Jenkins laid himself flat on his belly, and cried, 'Oh, Great Czar, do not punish me but give me permission to speak!' He thought he would do well to tell the Czar what he wanted to hear before he even had a chance to ask. 'I have news of Elixir, Great Czar! Demons have tell me – at last! – how to make! No doubt! I know, Great Czar!'

The Czar leaned forward.

Master Jenkins, who was straining his eyes upwards to see, even though his head was lowered, caught the movement. The Czar did not need to speak.

'Great Czar – do not punish me, I speak only what

demon say. Great Czar, demon say, Elixir must be made from – from blood and heart of boy borned on Christmas Day, and – '

The Czar reared back against his cushions and looked round, as if for his guards. 'One shall be found!'

'Great Czar, Great Czar, no need! My boy – Christian – he is call Christian because borned on Christmas Day. But, Czar – '

'You shall make the Elixir immediately,' said the Czar, and sat up straighter on his cushions. He seemed about to call for help.

Panic filled Master Jenkins with a mouse's frantic trembling. He must contradict the Czar. 'Czar, Great Czar, do not punish me but give me permission to speak – demon say more.'

'What?'

'Demon say, heart and blood of boy – and heart and blood of heavenly angel, Great Czar.'

It was what Master Jenkins had planned to say, and had laughed at his own cleverness in planning to say – but now that he had said it . . . The Czar drew back against his cushions and folded his arms across his chest. He said nothing, and the silence seemed enormous and long. Master Jenkins was in terror.

'The boy for young and strong, Great Czar,' he bleated, 'the angel for immortality. Is only way. Is what demon say.'

The Czar's fear – always greater than that of other men – swung him this way and that. If he killed the Angel, he feared the punishment of God and Hell – and yet he would be glad to be rid of the Angel. And the

Elixir – the Elixir offered him safety from death.

'This is why God send you Angel, Great Czar,' Master Jenkins said. 'God have such love for you, He wish you have Elixir. He send you Angel to make it.'

It was what the Czar wanted to hear: he could have the Elixir, be rid of the angel, and yet be sure of God's love – indeed, God's love for him was so great that He was willing to sacrifice an angel for Grozni's immortality!

Master Jenkins, glimpsing that smile, ducked his head and lay on the carpet in a warm, happy heap. Of those born to believe lies, the Czar was King. Into the Elixir would go Master Jenkins's only rival, the Black Angel; and also that boy Christian, who could tell so many embarrassing truths about his master. And he, Master Jenkins, would be the unsurpassed wizard who had given the Czar the Elixir of Immortality. No one would ever again be able to take his place of honour with the Czar. He would be able to persuade the Czar to do anything – and the northern lords would reward him with an estate. And the other courtiers would be grateful for the removal of the Black Angel. Then, before the Czar could change his mind again, back to England Master Jenkins would go as a rich foreign lord, and live happily ever after.

The Czar was sitting upright on his dais. 'How soon can it be made?'

Master Jenkins thought rapidly. 'Great Czar . . . I have boy . . . Bring me Angel . . . Bring me butchers . . . Tomorrow, Great Czar?'

'Today!' said the Czar, and rose from his dais. He

passed Master Jenkins with a breeze of his silk gowns and a gust of sour scent. A diamond slipped from a broken thread and fell before Master Jenkins's nose, glittering and turning the water in his eyes to stars. He heard the Czar clapping his hands and shouting at a distance and heaved himself to his knees – but not before picking up the diamond.

Today, he thought. Today he would have to turn Christian and that Black Angel fellow into Elixir. He had not thought it would be so soon.

Ah well, he thought, bracing his shoulders. A little unpleasant business to be got through before the pleasure could begin, like munching through the dreary turnips and black bread before getting to the cake. He stumped slowly to his feet and hurried after the Czar, eager to show how willing he was to make the Elixir.

In the normal way of things, it took hours for the Czar to get so much as a glass of small beer in his vast palace, for the order must be given to the guard, who passed it to another guard, who passed it to another, until it reached a private lowly enough to speak to a servant. And then the servant must take the order to the officer in charge of the kitchens, who passed it to his under-ling, who passed it to his, and so on until it reached a kitchen maid humble enough to actually take the jug to the barrel and fill it, and then pour some into a glass. And then the glass must be passed from her to her superior, and then to her superior, and so on until it reached the officer of the kitchen once more, and then he must carry it to the Czar's apartments, and seek permission from the guards to enter. And the guards must make sure that the Czar *had* ordered the beer, and then the officer would be allowed in – and by then, as like as not, the Czar no longer wanted the beer.

But when the Czar said, 'It will be done today', and went himself to demand that it was – well, then all ceremony was abandoned and things were done in a whirl.

In an hour – no, in less time than that – the necessary tools were found and brought to Master Jenkins's workroom, and soldiers were sent off to search the palace for the Angel.

While Christian, at his master's orders, was lighting the workroom candles in their bronze stands, in came the Czar, with his black-clothed guards. The Czar seated himself in his black chair, and the warm light glimmered on the gold wire and gems on his robes, and on the buckles and weapons of the guards.

Master Jenkins hurried to stand beside the Czar, and Christian, having lit all the candles, blew out his taper and watched curiously. Master Jenkins hadn't told him what was happening. They weren't going to raise a demon, or he would have been in his demon-suit and hidden in the hidey-hole. What, then? No magical signs or letters were chalked on the floor. Instead, at the centre of the circle of candlelight were two big, rough wooden tubs, such as were used at pig-killings. A large kitchen cleaver leaned in one, and coils of strong, hairy rope had been thrown down beside them.

Master Jenkins bent over the Czar and said, in a loud whisper, 'The Angel, Great Czar, the Angel!'

The Czar looked up at his Guard Captain, and the

Guard Captain's head snapped round as he looked towards the door. Everyone looked in the same direction and saw, coming in, more guards, carrying slung between them something long and limp. They carried it to the centre of the room and dumped it on the floor beside the wooden tubs. It was the Czar's Black Angel, seemingly in a deep sleep, if angels slept. Its eyes were closed, its arms sprawled where they had fallen; and its black, black hair, threaded with moon-white beads, spread over the wooden floorboards.

'Now,' Master Jenkins said to the soldiers.

The soldiers were all men who had grown up on farms. Every autumn, on those farms, pigs had been killed. The pigs were first bashed on the head with a sledgehammer, to stun them so they wouldn't struggle. Then, with ropes, they were slung up by the heels from an overhead beam. Their throats were cut, and the blood poured down into a wooden tub set underneath. From that blood the farm-women would make blood sausage and black pudding. From the blood of an angel and a boy, the Czar hoped to make the Elixir.

While Christian still stared and wondered, a soldier hefted a sledge and smashed its iron head down on his skull. Without a sound, Christian fell in a heap.

The other soldiers moved in with quick, neat movements. In no time at all they had Christian slung from a roof-beam by his heels. A wooden tub, smelling faintly of pickles, was kicked under the boy's dangling head. One of the soldiers, with a sharp knife and a single stroke, opened Christian's throat. Down the blood poured, steaming in the chill air of the room, splattering into the wooden tub, down and down it poured, filling the tub.

Master Jenkins watched it. He did not dare to look away, though he felt his feet tremble against the floor, and felt the shudders run upwards, through his knees, to shake his arms against his chest, his hands against his mouth. He felt his eyes would never close again, for fear of what pictures might form behind them. The smell of the blood reached into his throat. But as long as the Czar watched calmly, he did not dare to squeak or look away. And the Czar did watch calmly. The Czar had watched many executions, had seen much fear, much blood, much pain. The fear and pain of others proved his power and gave him pleasure. Only his own fear, his own pain, troubled him.

Half glancing at Master Jenkins, he said, 'We have the boy's blood.'

'Yes, Great Czar,' Master Jenkins managed, though he hardly had the breath. There seemed to be something so thick in his mouth – blood, perhaps? – that he could hardly speak.

Other soldiers had slung up the Angel beside Christian. 'We shall see the colour of an angel's blood,' the Czar said, as the soldier grasped, with a bloody hand, the black hair of the Angel.

And Master Jenkins noticed a fallen jewel glittering on the floor.

But what was it (asks the cat) that Shingebiss saw in Hel's black drink, in the Ghost World?

I shall tell you (says the cat) – though what of Christian?

When the eyes of Christian's body were blinded to this world, then the eyes of his spirit opened wide. But Christian was ignorant of the Ghost World, and the road to it. No one had sung to him of the way to follow. Hearing the voices of soldiers and glimpsing them moving around a hanging carcass, he took fright and, thinking himself still alive and in a body, ran from them – but his running took him not to anywhere he knew, but into darkness.

It was like being lost in the palace yards on a winter night, except that despite the cold, there was no chill snow-light, and no warmer light showed through any shutters. Everywhere he turned was more air and darkness, and more muttering and jostling of others passing. He spoke to them, asked where he was, but they – as lost as he – did not understand him, pushed him from their way and passed on – to where, they did not know.

Christian had stumbled among those many lost spirits who, not knowing the way to the Ghost World, and not being lucky enough to find it by chance, wander off among the many other worlds.

Here and there they find their way into one, and see a brief glimpse of light, and talk, and life – but they appear in those worlds as ghosts, arousing fear in those who see them – while in the ghosts is roused the pain of loss. And either they wander from that world into darkness again, or they stay and are slowly torn into fog by the buffets of the winds.

Poor Christian (says the cat). So much for his life.

9

Do you remember (asks the cat) how Shingebiss looked into the dark cup Hel offered her?

She looked into the dark drink and saw red, red . . .

She saw Christian's blood pouring into the wooden tub, and she saw her own body, hanging by its ankles.

She saw the soldier's hand, greasy with Christian's blood, grope for a hold in her own hair. She saw the light swim along the bloodied blade of the raised cleaver.

And she took no sip of the drink but, new shaman as she was, spirit as she was, threw herself into the sound of her own heartbeat. She returned across a world-wide gap with the speed of one wakening from a nightmare.

As the soldier's hand tightened in her hair, she opened her eyes and screamed at him in gyrfalcon rage, with staring, glowing gyrfalcon eyes – and such fright thrilled through him at the eerie sound, at the furious, staring eyes, that his body weakened, and he staggered back, and the cleaver dropped from his hand to chop into the floor.

It seemed that the Black Angel had become an angel indeed – or that a furious falcon bated at the end of the rope. White wings thrashed the gauzy candlelight into tatters – the breeze from the wings blew out candles and brought darkness dropping from the rafters. And the bird's shriek, its furious, wild, icicle shriek – *Keeee-ya! Keeee-ya!* – stabbed ears and fluttered hearts and echoed from the wooden walls. The ropes that had held Shingebiss could not hold the gyrfalcon. They fell from it, and it flew free, screeching, in the air of the room.

Words have power. Even when used by people with no skill in witchcraft, no shamanry, words can alter sight and make things appear other than they are.

Music has power. Even when made by people with no skill in witchcraft, no shamanry, music has power to change the beat of blood.

When a witch uses words and music, their power is greater. But when a shaman, who has passed through the Ghost World Gate and returned, when a shaman twines words and music together and uses them with a shaman's power, then nothing that hears can resist, and even rope must wriggle to the shaman's wishes.

The gyrfalcon gyring among the rafters made a wild and raucous music, but its song of fury and hatred and fear entered in at every ear, and thrashed and pierced in every body. The black-clothed soldiers who had butchered a helpless boy – these soldiers' hearts fluttered as fast as the falcon's wings beat. Their guts quivered within them; their whole bodies trembled. They fell to the floor and crawled for the door, but curled into balls, sobbing and pissing themselves with terror before they reached it.

The Czar was pinned in his place by fear. Every shriek of the falcon was a long steel pin that pierced him through and sank deep into the chair behind him. The Czar's eyes stared, his mouth hung open and dribble ran down into his beard. His piss steamed and stained his silk robes.

Master Jenkins, sunk to his knees, leaned against the Czar's chair and leaned his head on its arm for support. His eyes were tight shut, and every shriek of the falcon rippled through his flesh, crying to him in Christian's voice. His whole body shuddered so hard that he thumped and thumped against the chair and the floor.

Only the Czar, his eyes fixed open with fear, saw the bird swoop down and, in mid-air, throw up its wings and drop to the floor as the Black Angel. With black hair wild and flung in fine nets across its furious face, the Angel turned on its heel as it struck the floor and glared at the Czar.

The Czar was transfixed as though by the wrath of Heaven. His jaw moved in jerks and from his mouth came a whimpering, such as a cat makes when it sees birds it cannot reach: 'Ah-ah-ah-ah-ah.' (Perhaps his terror was as great as that of the many executed at his order? But how can terror be measured; who could do the measuring?) The Czar wanted to turn his head, to look for the soldiers who should be protecting him, but he could not move his head. He could not move his eyes, or his hands which gripped the chair's arms. He tried to speak Master Jenkins's name instead, but could not shape his lips to form the words.

It would have done no good. Master Jenkins could not lift his head from the arm of the Czar's chair. And the soldiers sobbed and grovelled on the floor in their own terror.

Christian's body still hung above the tub filled with his blood, and the Czar watched as the Black Angel turned to it. The Angel made a calm study of the poor, dangling corpse, but studied it long and well. The air of the high dark room quivered with the memory of the falcon's shrieks, and under that quivering was the slight creaking of the rope that held the corpse, the quiet snivelling of the soldiers, and the Czar's 'Ah-ah-ah-ah-ah.'

The Angel spun on its heel. 'Jenkins,' it said, 'lift up your head.' And Master Jenkins lifted his head as if he were a puppet and his head had been lifted on a string.

'Grozni,' said the Angel to the Czar. The Angel's voice was as quiet as the rope's creaking. They heard every word. 'You wish to live for ever? I promise you, Grozni, you will not die. And you, Jenkins – ' As the terrifying Angel stepped closer, Master Jenkins tried to cower closer to the chair, to lower his head and hide his eyes. But he could not lower his head. 'You wish to call demons, Jenkins? You wish to be a man of power?' The Angel lowered its face close to his. Its hair fell about him and at the touch of the hair Jenkins's flesh leaped with fear as if he had been scalded. 'You shall see a calling, Jenkins. You shall see the calling of a *true* power.'

Suddenly – and Master Jenkins yelped with fright – the Angel pushed its hand into the opening of his robe and touched his plump and sweaty chest. The Angel looked into his blue eyes with its own hard, black eyes, as it felt the frantic thumping and stumbling of his heart. 'It may kill you,' the Angel said, and withdrew its hand, and stood back. Its long hair withdrew from Jenkins's clothes and sweaty face, and he was left, exhausted, sweating, slumped against the Czar's chair – and indeed, his heart swayed and thumped and leaped in him so wildly that he could hardly breathe and felt at his last gasp.

The Angel walked to the centre of the circle that – smudged and faded – could still be seen drawn on the wooden floor. There, in the flickering light of the few candles left alight, in the shadow of Christian's hanging carcass, beside the wooden tub of boy's blood, Shingebiss began to sing.

From her single throat, two or even three voices seemed to rise: deep, swaying notes that seemed to hum from every corner of the room, stirring the air and the darkness. And a higher, sweeter voice that wove around and about the deeper voices, spiralling up into the rafters. But this was not one of those lullabies that had soothed the Czar. This was a freezing, barbed song whose words locked the listeners' joints and held them, as in a trap.

Then Shingebiss's song began to call. Up and up rose the silver notes, striving and striving to reach the one called. On and on hummed the deep notes, sinking into the earth, calling, calling.

Again and again the call went up, went out, until to those cowering on the floor, and against the chair, and in the chair, it was pain. They felt the call in their bones; it ached in their skulls, called and pulled at their vitals; it seemed to be tugging the hearts from their breasts.

They felt it pulling at the muscles and cords of their own throats. Against their wills, though they clenched their teeth, they found themselves calling too.

The call reached beyond the workroom that housed it. Birds flying in the black and icy dark above the roof reeled in their flight and spun downwards. Cats and foxes, hurrying secretly through the cold of the palace yards, turned aside and came to the call. Guards lifted their heads and stood listening, though to what, or for what, they couldn't tell. Sleepers gasped as they missed a breath and turned in their beds to face the call.

But this call had to reach beyond the borders of the world. Shingebiss had no ghost drum to beat, and make wings of the drum-beat to carry her call. She began to dance, and made the drumming with her heels on the wooden floor, and with the clapping of her hands. And *Keeee-ya!* She sent out the piercing, insistent call of the falcon.

And still, still her call was not strong enough. Anyone can call the powers, but will they come when called? How to win their favour, who need no favours? How to pique their curiosity, who have dreamed all?

'Call!' she said, and from the throats of Master Jenkins and from the Czar himself came screams of pure terror, echoing, helplessly, calling to them something they feared to see. From their huddles on the floor the soldiers rose, grimed with dust and blood, and they screamed.

And Shingebiss could half see, behind her eyes, the turning head . . . She could hear the listening of the thing she called . . . And she could feel that still it would not come, not yet, not yet . . .

She danced, she pleaded, she falcon-called, with all her strength and all her hope . . . As she danced, gasping and breathless, she spun down and dipped her hand into the thickening blood in the tub. With bloodied fingers, she striped her own face. The blood seeped into her mouth, and the iron taste was on the tongue that made the call: come, come, come, come . . .

She spun in her dance and kicked at the tub; she stooped and wrenched at it, and over went the tub. Out poured and spread the sluggish blood, black in the candlelight, carrying blacker clots. Slowly, thickly, it spread to touch the soldiers, it spread to the Czar's feet, it spread around Master Jenkins's knees. Its stench rose up and filled the room, and was carried on the call. Out in the cold, the eyes of the gathering cats and foxes gleamed. They licked their chops. Soldiers shuddered at their posts; sleepers woke suddenly.

And Shingebiss danced in the blood, splashing her boots and leggings, stamping the blood through the floorboards, where it dripped to the waiting cats, the waiting foxes, in the yard.

Keeee-ya! She felt the lurch of the world, the opening of its borders. What she called was coming. Exhausted, gasping, the sweat running down her in streams, she sank to a crouch on the blood-sticky floor and she shivered, her legs trembling under her. The soldiers, Jenkins, the Czar, all stopped their screaming and waited, as frozen still as frightened rabbits. They too could feel the coming, and they feared it.

The air of the room tightened. It dragged on their skins, drawing out their hairs, shivering across their skins; tightened around their heads until their heads ached. It was too heavy to drag into their lungs, and left them hollow and choking.

And cold. Despite the braziers pouring out their heat, despite the candles that still burned, the draughts that blew into the room grew sharper and chiller, and the sweat on their bodies turned icy.

The dark red light of the braziers and the little yellow crocus flowers of the candle-flames burned bright and brighter as the darkness thickened about them. Master Jenkins stared at the brightness, holding it with his eyes, praying that it would not be smothered by the rising dark.

Then, carried on the cold draughts, an animal whiff, a stink of wet fur, growing stronger and thicker, and stronger, as the room became colder and darker. Shingebiss alone knew the stink for the stink of an otter, and by that stink she knew the one she had called had come. She waited, crouching in the thickening stain of Christian's blood. She breathed hard, waiting.

A breeze seemed to blow through her head, shivering her thoughts, shivering her sight, as a reflection in a still pool shivers when the wind blows over the water. The breeze blew again, more strongly, and her sight turned black, blind; and her nose filled with the stink of otter until she could smell nothing else, not even the blood.

And then she felt a new hardness and strength in her legs, her arms. Her legs pushed and she stood straight, and her body towered. Though still sightless, she felt the closeness of the roof-beams to her head. She stretched out her arms, and her fingers, and felt claws flick out from her fingertips. There was a shagginess of fur hanging about her. She opened her eyes and saw and saw and saw.

She saw the darkness of the room and its burning, dying candles; its little, cowering figures. She saw beyond its walls, to the dark outside, the stars, the snow. She saw the palace, and its many rooms, and its many people; its lurking spiders and running mice. Beyond that, she saw, or felt, the city and all its life, awake and asleep; and beyond that, the open country, the forest, the wolves and the deer; the distant towns, the villages . . . And she saw the day that was to come, and the day that had been, and the summer that was to come, and the summer that had been . . . She saw all at once, without confusion, as, on a sunny day, you can see the water of a lake, and the fish beneath it, and the reflected mountains above it, and the reflected sky and clouds above that, without ever moving your eyes or head.

She had called Loki, the First Shaman, Baldur's brother; and Loki had come, had sent his spirit into her. She was Loki.

Loki-Shingebiss brought her gaze back from the world's edges, and directed it at the small people at her feet. She saw their short pasts, and their shorter futures. She said, 'Jenkins! Demon-Master!'

Master Jenkins heard the call, and closed his eyes more tightly. The stink had thickened to a choking foulness, so he hardly dared to take a breath, and his heart beat so fast, it hurt. But the voice called his name again, and he had to open his eyes.

He saw a shape forming out of the haze of candlelight and darkness, a shape that grew more solid and, creeping, crouching, came towards him. It was a demon. Not such a demon as he had called from his cupboard. This demon was covered, not in red velvet, but in rank black fur which gleamed in the light, slick with grease or some wetness – though, in places, it was tufted and glued with filth.

As it came, the toes of its feet spread and gripped the wooden floor, and its talons bit into the wood. Its arms reached out to him, and they were long arms, too long, ridged with muscle and sinew under the fur. From its finger-ends slid long claws, which slid out of sight again as the fingers bent, like a cat's claws.

Around its legs there coiled a long tail, bare of fur, and ringed like a worm, lashing with all a worm's muscular strength.

The choking stink came from its mouth, from between its wet, yellow teeth: the stench of old meat, the breath of a meat-eater.

Master Jenkins calmly watched it come. His fear was so immense that it seemed everything, and he was no longer aware of it any more than he was aware of everything. His heart had beaten so hard for so long that it seemed a pain he had always known. He did not try to rise, or to run. He knew that he could not run. As the thing came closer, he raised his head to keep its toothed, gaping face, its mad tiger's eyes always in his sight. The hairs of his head and beard were pulled towards it, pulling at his skin with a tiny prickling that seemed greater than the pain of his heart.

And then, as the demon stood above him and bent over him, he realized, with a shock, that he had been mistaken; the candlelight and darkness had confused his eyes. It was Christian who stooped over him. And, looking up in amazement, Master Jenkins thought he saw Christian beginning a red smile – but lower than a smile should be.

Master Jenkins's heart, lunging to a yet faster beat, foundered, and stopped. He toppled sideways, thumping on the wooden floor, and lay dead.

His eyes were blinded to this world for ever, but the eyes of the spirit within him opened wide, wider than they had ever done in his dreams.

That spirit looked about it – and still saw the demon in the firelight. Master Jenkins had been taught all about Heaven and Hell, and demons and angels, while he had been alive, but he had believed in none of them. Now he believed that he was in Hell, and would be punished for his disbelief. In terror, his spirit ran away, and left its body, and this world, behind.

Master Jenkins knew nothing of the Ghost World, nor of the road to it. He fled into darkness, and was lost. He found himself among voices without bodies. The voices passed him by on either side, sighing and muttering, speaking unknown words. Master Jenkins called out to them, he tried to catch them by the arm – but when he reached into the darkness, he found no one there.

'Christian!' he called into the darkness. 'Christian!'

On he went, into the darkness, fearing at every step

to fall into a pit, or strike his face against a wall, or run into the arms and claws of a bear. 'Christian! Christian!' From the darkness, nothing answered him.

Loki-Shingebiss withdrew her gaze from the darkness where Master Jenkins's spirit had vanished, and looked down at the Czar.

And the Czar, still seated, frozen, in his chair, thought that a mirror had appeared before him. He saw himself, the Czar Grozni, his pointed beard and his oiled ringlets, his glittering, shimmering robes and his white face above them.

But not a mirror image, for it stood while he sat and, as he pressed himself against the back of his chair, he watched the flesh of his own face shrink back from his teeth, saw the flesh shrivel from the nose-holes and eye-holes of his own skull. The Czar's feet pushed against the floor, his hands pushed against the chair-arms, and he had no sound to make as he watched what he feared most of all: his own death and decay. Was the Czar more afraid than those he had sent to execution? The Czar had no thought for them.

The Czar watched his own living skull laugh at him; and then he saw the figure that stood above him shift and change. It was no longer a skeleton dressed in Czar's robes, nor a demon, nor Christian, nor even the slight Black Angel.

It grew tall and wide and – strange. From it came a strong animal stink, and the set of its head on its thick, ruffed neck was not human. Its face, its mask . . . snouted, shaggy, and its dark eyes glistened in their settings. The candlelight shone on sleek fur, caught goldenly on coarse guard hairs – but was it the fur of a coat put on, or a coat grown? The Czar, staring, helpless, was almost dead from fear.

Then the creature that watched him reached out and grasped the front of his robe. Its nails pierced and tore the silk and it lifted his weight from the chair; its grip snapped wires and scattered jewels. Pearls, rubies, emeralds, diamonds fell pattering to the floor – but Master Jenkins's ears did not hear.

When the Czar was sagging on his feet, the creature twisted, like a miller heaving a sack to his back, and threw the Czar over its shoulder. The Czar hung as limp as any meal-filled sack.

And then the creature, who was Loki, the First Shaman, who was Shingebiss, who was Loki-Shingebiss, walked away into the Northlands. The walls of the palace were not there; the streets of the city were not there. The First Shaman's eyes looked, and saw and saw and saw: saw everything that had been, and was, and much that would be. To the First Shaman, stone walls ten feet thick, which had stood for three hundred years, were as frail as mist. And with one step the First Shaman could step from dream to dream, from world to world, and weave in and out of them.

After three strides Loki-Shingebiss stood in the Northlands forest. The Czar was dropped in the snow and lay, face down, unmoving. Above him was the black, freezing sky that he had so seldom seen. Around him the dark pine branches moved in the wind, and murmured loud, a sound like a sea, a sound like heavy rain that never falls; a sound that would have terrified the Czar if he had not been too far gone in terror to care.

Loki-Shingebiss straightened her back and stood straight, and her head was among the treetops with their long, moaning rustle. She looked up, and the bright, icy spikes of the stars seemed just above her head. She looked down and saw the forest spread at her feet, looked into its clearings, saw the twisting lines of its frozen streams and rivers. She saw, all at once, a forest busy with growing and living and killing, where a human hunter had been the rarest of its animals; and a forest where whole hillsides were striped with felled trunks, and where the meat and skins of deer, wolves, lynx and beaver hung on gallows, to freeze, beside the hunters' camps. She saw the end of Balder's dreaming: a forest of stumps and desolation, from which the animals, finding no shelter and little food, had fled if they had not been killed; a forest from which, in the spring thaw, the rivers and streams carried away the soil no longer held by the tree-roots . . . Oh, the North-lands, the Northlands are barren and bare; no seed-time, no harvest is ever known there. Are you cold, my children?

Loki-Shingebiss sat on the snow and looked at the dark shapes of two trees that grew with a space between them too narrow for a man to bridge with his spread arms. And then, beating taloned hands on her she began to sing.

To Shingebiss, lost within the power of the First Shaman, it was as if she dreamed, knowing what she must do without thought. Lost within a huge and powerful shell, she moved with it, did as it wished. The walking had taxed her bones and her joints until they seemed ready to break under her, had forced her heart to beat its utmost; and now the singing opened and stretched her lungs until each new breath was like swallowing a sword. But she sang with joy, loving the strength, loving the sight that showed her past and future. And if her heart, like Master Jenkins's must beat until it failed, then so it must be.

The song was of the Ghost World Gate. Shingebiss listened in wonder as her mouth shaped words she had never known: a long song-story that told of the Gate, its black wood, aged to iron; that told of its strange hinges, which let it open any way it was pushed; of how it stood across the road to the Ghost World, barring the world of the living from the world of the dead. And despite Shingebiss's breathless pain, the song went on, to tell of the long ages when there had been no death in this world, and how, during all that age, the Gate had stood shut – 'Until I, Loki, until I, First Shaman, until I shaped the mistletoe dart, and brought death to Balder!'

The song called down to Earth the power that rushed through the tree branches above. The sound of the wind quietened, and a darkness darker than the winter began to form between the tree-trunks. The darkness thickened and thickened and, by the time the story was told of how the Ghost World Gate had first opened for Balder, the first of the dead, and then for Loki, the First Shaman, there was a gate standing in the Northlands forest, between the two fir trees.

The song ended and, lost within the strength of Loki-Shingebiss, Shingebiss slumped. She tried to draw air into sore lungs, and her heart beat wildly, dizzying her head with the pumping of blood. Every part of her ached with the strain of the power that flowed through her, and she was dying, she was sure, she was dying.

But now she rose and walked through the trees with stretching strides that wrenched at her joints. She reached high into the trees and tore down great heavy branches; stooped and reached into the snow, which melted at her touch, and gathered, from the earth pine cones.

These branches and pine cones she carried back to the Gate and, at her approach, the Gate swung open on to darkness. Through it she flung all that she carried. And then she went to the Czar, who still lay huddled and hardly alive on the snow, and she grasped his robe in one hand and lifted him and carried him with her as she stepped through the Gate.

And there, in the Ghost World, at the edge of Iron Wood, in sight of Hel's palace, Loki-Shingebiss stuck the branches into the Ghost World's earth, and crushed the pine cones in her hands and scattered the seeds. She began to sing again, though it seemed to Shingebiss that the words scored her throat like knives, and that each rib was tearing from her backbone. The song sang of the trees that the seeds and the branches could be. It described them: their scent, their leaves, their cones, the insects that lived in their bark. Each tree was pictured in her mind, full-grown, clear; and her whole will was that the tree should become what she wished. Strength poured out of her into the trees, and the branches took root and grew upwards;

and the seeds sprouted and grew and grew.

And when all were full-grown, the song was not finished, but went on and on, calling on the trees to flower, fruit and shed their seed, calling on the new seedlings to grow until there was, in the Ghost World, a forest, not of iron trees such as have always grown there, but trees of our world, trees of bark and wood and sap. A beautiful forest of dark firs and white birch, rising into the endless twilight of the Ghost World.

And then Loki-Shingebiss went to the open Gate between the worlds, and seating herself there and beating on her knees with her hands, she began yet another song, a song of calling, a ghost song, summoning every bird, every animal, every insect, sleeping or waking, that made its home in the Northlands forest.

They came to the call: they could not help but come. A winter wolf-pack, grey and white as the winter, came through the trees of our world in a quick, gliding run, and passed through the Gate, passed by the shaman and vanished into the forest she had made for them. They went silently, as if on the hunting trail. A summer wolf-pack followed them, carrying in their coats many summer seeds, which fell in the Ghost World forest and sprouted where the firs would let them.

The ghost song went on. Out of the Northlands forest of this world it called a reindeer stag and his herd of does; and four tall bony elk, their antlers shed for the winter. And then summer herds, carrying summer seeds on their coats and in their bellies, all to be dropped in the Ghost World forest. And when they had obeyed the song and passed through the Gate, there came scurrying over the surface of the snow scores of the small lemmings and voles, rats and mice who filled the forest; and scores more of the red squirrels and hares. Many of them were called, for their small bodies would have to feed the animals who followed: the skinny, hungry marten, the sable, the foxes, the shambling glutton, the men and the women, and their children.

The song had special words for the women who came carrying, as the song told them, water in cups. And when they had passed through the Gate, and were in the Ghost World forest, these women spilt their water on the ground, some here, some there, and from that spilt water ran streams and rivers of the same water that ran on Earth. If the forest had been watered by the Ghost World's rusty streams, the trees would soon all have turned to iron.

And still the song went on, though Shingebiss was past exhaustion, and was using, not her own strength, but the strength of the power that filled her. Her throat felt cracked, her chest broken, and breathing was pain. But still she sang, calling the snow-owls and the ptarmigan, and all the many, many summer birds: the robins and the geese, the ducks and the sparrows, the starlings and thrushes and finches.

And when they had all flown through the Gate, bringing with them seeds, then, at last, there was one more word to sing.

At that word, the Gate swung shut, and, in this world, vanished. Where it had stood were two split and blasted fir trees.

The power of the wind rushed into the treetops again, swaying them, brushing branches of pine needles against each other, making trunks creak and groan in a great wondering murmur beneath the black and silver sky.

10

But in the Ghost World (asks the cat)?

The Ghost World is no bigger, and yet it holds more than it once did.

It holds Iron Wood, with its steel-thorned briars and rusty streams and, lost deep in Iron Wood, overgrown with sharp thorns, it holds Hel's palace.

And now too it holds a living forest of fir and birch. Streams of earthly water run through these trees, and if the water is amber brown, then it's not with rust. Living animals come to drink at these streams, deer and wolves both; and many birds bathe in the shallows.

In Iron Wood the sleepers wake at the sound of a living wolf's howl, and the lullaby Hel sings for Balder is broken by the singing of a living thrush. Even in the Ghost World, only change is everlasting.

Seated cross-legged in the forest, Loki-Shingebiss whistled, and to her hand came a bird. She reached up and broke, from a tree, a dry brown twig, close-grown with green spines and holding a single, old, empty cone. She whistled again, and the bird sprang from her hand and flew away.

It flew through the Northlands forest, and into Iron Wood. It flew to Hel's palace and in at a window. It flew to Balder's bed, and let the twig fall on to his pillow, where, in a moment of half-sleep, his hand found it.

And, when the bird returned without the twig, Loki-Shingebiss had no more songs to sing. The spirit of Loki withdrew into its own dream, and left her.

The withdrawing was like the withdrawing of water from a lake-bed, which then dries and cracks. It was like the withdrawing of water from a herb, which then wilts and falls.

Shingebiss fell back into the earth of the forest she had made, so exhausted, so senseless, she could not even feel the pain of her driven body.

As she lay sleeping, wolves came out of the forest and gathered near her. They lay in the shelter of young trees, and laid their heads on their paws; or they sat upright with ears pricked and tongues lolling; and they waited.

And, as Shingebiss lay sleeping, the Czar Grozni stirred in the daze of bewilderment and fear. The ground beneath him seemed hard and real. There was, around him, a quiet, constant sound of rustling and rushing, like running water or the dragging over the rushes of a long gown. The Czar thought it was the sound of his palace fountains, but dared not raise his head and look for a long time. There came no louder sound, and nothing touched him. He slowly lifted his head and looked about.

And found himself in a forest, at dusk. Newly terrified, he scrabbled in the pine needles with hands and toes, and got to his feet. He stumbled to a tree, and felt its ridged bark beneath his hands, and felt its bark-dust itch between his fingers. The forest was real. He turned himself about and about, looking for a palace – or, if not a palace, then a hunting lodge, even a house, a hut. Or a wagon, or a road, or some sign that men and women were near.

He saw nothing but trees, tall, straight pine trees, their dark branches darkening the air until, at a short distance, even the dusk turned to full dark between them. My enemies, he thought, have brought me here, and left me, to starve. But he didn't remember being brought there. I have been drugged, he thought. My enemies have taken my throne. And he thought wildly of Pavel, whom he had executed, and Pavel's family, and many, many other traitors there had been. Perhaps, he thought, they are hiding in the forest to kill me like a wild animal. And he moved nervously away from the place where he had woken, fearing to be found there.

After a few steps, he stopped again, for he had seen something new: not a tree, nor a fallen branch, but a long fall of black hair lying stretched across the pine needles; black hair decorated with moon-white bone-beads. And a face, under the hair, but turned away from the Czar. It was the Black Angel.

Another step, and the Czar saw the Black Angel lying as if dead, as if thrown down on the ground, with arms and legs sprawled. And now there rushed into the Czar's mind a memory of the Black Angel screaming like a falcon, and changing before his eyes into a demon. The Czar spun around, his muscles already moving to run; and then he froze, and turned again, so suddenly that he came to his knees in the pine needles.

He stared at the Black Angel, lying there, so still; and he looked about for something he could use to smash in the Angel's hateful head: a stone, a log ... Seeing nothing, he thought that perhaps he could use his fists, but quickly, quickly, before the thing woke ...

But as he made the first, slightest move towards the Angel, he heard a low snickering growl; and he saw something move. A wolf, that had been hidden by a young fir, got to its feet, its ears laid back, its lips wrinkled above white teeth. And there was another, and another, darker grey in the grey of the dusk. The Czar turned, twisted to his feet, and ran, and, thinking the wolves were bounding after him with their terrible strength, he ran harder and more and more wildly, veering around trees, striking them and falling to the ground, scrambling up and looking behind, and running on, jumping streams and landing in them, wading out and running on.

The wolves had not followed him. They had lain down, on each side of Shingebiss, and laid their noses on their paws.

When the Czar could run no further, he collapsed in the pine needles, but, though he gasped and heaved painfully for breath, his fear did not allow him to rest. Always he turned his head, straining his eyes to peer into the dark, straining his senses to hear every sound there might be. He was afraid of enemies who were hunting him, he was afraid of wolves and bears; he was even afraid of the ghosts and forest demons that must haunt this place.

As soon as he could, he got on his feet and went on,

looking and looking for people who would serve him. His robes were already ripped. Now they were torn further, and stained by dirt and old pine needles; draggled in streams. He found nothing to eat, for he knew only how to hunt on horseback with a spear or gun and hundreds of attendants to drive the animals towards him. Hunger was a sharp pain, and then a sickness, and then an ache, but though he grew starved, he didn't die; and he struggled on.

He found people. He heard the sound of axes and struggled towards it, and found people felling trees. He made his way to a tree-stump and sat down on it, and waited for them to come and kiss his feet and ask what they might do for him.

The people ignored him. As they went on working, they gave him a glance or two. The Czar would not look at them.

In time, they stopped work, and sat among the fallen trees themselves, and unpacked bread, meat and cheese from bags they had with them. One of them called out to the Czar, but the Czar would not look at them or answer them. He was the Czar, and they must come and bow down to him. Something fell close by his feet. It was a lump of sausage, thrown to him by one of the tree-fellers. The Czar's mouth watered, and before he could stop himself, he had picked the sausage up and was eating it. And the men laughed at him. Furious, the Czar rose and stood straight, thinking to order the men's punishment – and then he realized that he was alone. He had no black-clothed soldiers around him to carry out his orders. And he looked down at himself, and saw that he was filthy and ragged, and held a lump of greasy sausage in his hand.

As the men went on laughing, the Czar crept back into the trees. But he carried the sausage with him and gnawed it as he went.

He stumbled on a track, followed it and came to the village that was being built with the felled trees. There too the people stared at him, but not in fear, and no one prostrated themselves on the ground before him. 'What do you want?' a woman called to him, and he could not answer for fury and shame. He did not know how to answer. All his life people had come to him, and had given to him. He did not know how to go to people and ask for what he wanted. He stood at the edge of the forest and glared at the women and the children and the men as they worked on their village.

A woman came to him and brought him a bowl of broth and a lump of fat to dip in it. He took it from her and ate it, vile though he thought it. And then he threw the bowl on the ground and went back into the forest.

He stayed close by the village, because someone always gave him something to eat, but he hated the people and he wanted to kill them. He watched the children, and he thought of carrying one away into the forest and killing it – but he was afraid, because he had no black-clothed soldiers to do it for him, or to protect him when the parents came searching. And so he lived, in the Ghost World.

The people of the village, who did not know they were in the Ghost World, thought him mad. 'Don't

wander into the forest, or the Wild Man will get you,'
they told their children.

'How does he keep alive?' they asked each other.
'He's starved to the bone; he never keeps alive on
what we give him.'

'He's a madman,' they said. 'He's a werewolf – have
you seen him bare his teeth? Have you seen him
glower?'

The people feared the forest. It was haunted. Out of
it came not only the madman, the werewolf, but
others, strangers in strange clothes, who came among
the people and asked their names. They seemed half
asleep, these strangers, and spoke of ancient times as
if they had lived them.

'Ghosts,' said the villagers, and wondered what else
lived in the forest around them.

The ghosts had come wandering from Iron Wood,
and had drunk from the streams of earthly water.
Then they had looked around and seen living trees,
and had remembered their life in our world. Poor
ghosts; finding the villagers afraid of them, and
remembering all too sharply the pains and disappoint-
ments of their lives, they went back through the forest
until they came once more on iron trees. They stooped
and drank of the rusty streams, and forgot life and
slept.

The Czar followed them, and he too came among
the iron trees, and he too bent and drank from the
rusty streams. Then he forgot that he had been a Czar
and God on Earth. He forgot Earth. He lay down
beneath an iron tree, and slept and dreamed – and

such dreams as he had may tell us why there is so much cruelty in our world.

And Shingebiss (says the cat): is she still sleeping?

So exhausted was she that she slept the year round. The trees around her flowered and fruited and added another year to their girth. The wolves hunted and ate, and came back to her, carrying food for those they had left on guard, as wolves do. But this was the Ghost World, and though the earthly forest growing within its borders may flower and fruit, there is no time in the Ghost World. Shingebiss might have slept through twenty, or fifty, seedings, and still not have been one moment older when she woke.

She woke in pain. The strength and power of the spirit that had ridden her had stretched and wrenched every joint almost to the parting of its sinews. It had used and torn and bruised every muscle of her back, her legs, her arms; every small muscle that covered her ribs, every muscle that rooted in her belly, every muscle was sore and stiff. There was no movement, not even the smallest, that did not hurt. And one arm would not move at all, the bone having cracked under the strain. But when, despite the pain, she lifted her head and looked around her at the forest, she was glad.

The wolves rose from beside her and moved away through the trees. She watched them go, and she was glad. She saw a red squirrel hanging upside down on the bark of a pine, and she was glad. A mouse scurried over the pine needles a finger's breadth from her hand, and she was very glad. What she had set out to do, she had done. She had saved the Northlands. Whatever destruction was worked on them in any other world, here, in the Ghost World, they would live.

In pain she struggled to sit and then, though it hurt to sing, she sang a song of healing. She set her good hand over the broken bone, and she sang it whole. And lay down and slept again.

The second time she woke, she still hurt, but not so much. Limping, she went to find a stream and, coming on one, disturbed an elk, which had been eating water plants, with its whole head under water. Hearing her, it threw up its great head, scattering showers of water about it, and lumbered off. Shingebiss was so glad to see the elk that she sat down by the water and laughed, though laughing hurt. She drank from cupped hands, and then sang another song, crooning to herself, which eased her aches. Lying by the stream, she dozed, and went spirit-travelling.

Where did she go (asks the cat)? Listen, and I'll tell you.

11

You must see (says the cat) a long, high room, floored and panelled in wood. In the middle of the floor is drawn, in smudged and fading chalk, a circle. At the edge of this circle is a tall bronze stand of many candles, but only a few are still burning, and their light now flares, now fades, glimmering on the bronze of their stand, glimmering on a wooden panel. From the rafters above, dark shadows hang down; from the corners, darkness pushes forward.

The air is moved by a sound of shuddering and sobbing. Hardly seen in the darkness, dressed as they are all in black, men are lying, hiding their faces, sobbing with fear into their arms.

On one side of the smudged circle, at the very edge of the shadows, hardly touched by the candlelight, is a great wooden chair. Little pinpoints of brilliant light shine on its seat and on the floor at its clawed wooden feet – fallen jewels. Beside the chair, on the floor, is a dark lump in the darkness. It lies very still. It doesn't sob or shudder.

Almost at the centre of the circle, in the full of what faint light there is, hangs Christian's body. Its dead weight makes it hang still. No sobbing comes from Christian.

The stink of blood in that room is very strong.

Master Jenkins's workroom (says the cat) is just as he left it when he died. But, in the world of the workroom, there has been no time to make changes. Time in the Ghost World runs sometimes slow, sometimes fast, but never at the same rate as in our world.

Shingebiss, in spirit, hung in the candlelight and shifted with the breath of the candles, into the darkness and into the light again. Wherever she drifted, she was unseen. She waited and watched.

At the far end of the room, the door rattled in its frame, and was then pushed open, scraping against the floor, making a loud noise that cracked through the darkness. The snivelling soldiers started up with cries.

In through the door came a cold wind, ruffling the candles and making the light dance higher on the walls and over the rafters. Two candles blew out, and the darkness dropped down a little further from the roof, pushed in a little nearer from the corners.

The door opened wider, and in came another troop of black-clothed soldiers, wearing swords and carrying pikes. They stopped short at the sight of their fellows wallowing in tears on the floor. 'On your feet, soldiers!' cried the Lieutenant in command, in a shout that echoed from the wooden walls. 'Attention!'

Only one of the soldiers tried to obey. He got to his knees, but then the shadow of Christian's body fell across him, cast by a flaring of a candle. The soldier flinched, and sprawled again on the floor, hiding his face.

'Search!' said the Lieutenant; and the newcomers

advanced into the candlelight, and into the shadows. Pikes held before them, they went into the furthest corners and returned slowly.

The Lieutenant walked to the hanging corpse and studied it. In the service of Czar Grozni, he had seen many like it. He looked at the circle drawn on the floor, at the stand of candles, at the blood-stained floor and the overturned tub.

'Lieutenant,' said a soldier. He was standing by the Czar's chair, pointing his pike at something on the floor. The Lieutenant brought a candle from the stand, and, by its light, saw that the thing on the floor was the body of a stout old man.

'It's the Czar's wizard, sir,' the soldier whispered.

The Lieutenant prodded the wizard's body with the toe of his boot. The wizard did not blink or move.

'Is he dead?'

The soldier, holding his pike upright, crouched and felt at Master Jenkins's throat and chest. 'Cold as a frozen fish, Lieutenant; dead as a dried one.'

'Where,' asked the Lieutenant, 'is the Czar?'

He walked back to the fallen soldiers, and tried to drag one of them to his feet, but the man whimpered, and made himself heavy, and would not stand. The Lieutenant crouched beside him. 'Where is the Czar?'

In answer, the man babbled, and sobbed, and whined. 'Gone!' he said, and 'Taken!'

The Lieutenant rose to his feet. 'You, rouse the guard. You, you, stay here on guard. The rest, with me!'

So began a search of the palace which entered every

building, every yard. Every church and chapel, every noble's apartment, every kitchen, every workshop, every dormitory, every stable, every storeroom. Every cellar underground, every tiny room in every tower.

And when that search didn't find the Czar, there began the search of the city.

The soldiers who had been found in the workroom, with the bodies of the wizard and his boy, were questioned. Where was the Czar? Had they murdered him? Come now, confess; they had murdered him, hadn't they?

They were allowed no rest to recover from their fear; their colleagues in the Czar's guard despised their tears and their cowardice; despised them for not guarding the Czar. When they could give no sensible answer to the questions, they were punched, knocked down, kicked. 'Answer! You murdered the Czar, didn't you? Why? You chopped his sacred body into pieces and buried it, like a dog's, in the yard, didn't you? Answer!'

And when the answer was no, no – then they were not merely beaten, but tortured. 'Come now, tell the truth. The pain will stop if you answer truthfully. You murdered the Czar, didn't you?'

No, said the soldiers, at different times, to their different torturers. A demon had come. The Czar and his wizard had been calling up a demon. They had sacrificed the wizard's boy to call up the demon, and the demon had come and it had slung the Czar over its back like a sack and carried him away to Hell. That was the truth. That was why his body was nowhere to be found. He was in Hell, with the Devil.

So they told what they knew of the truth; but their torturers said, 'Liars! Liars still! You murdered the Czar, didn't you?'

So they stopped telling the truth, and said, 'Yes! Yes, we killed the Czar – now stop hurting us.'

But the torturers didn't stop. Now they said, 'Tell us how you killed him. Tell us where you've put the body. Tell us why you killed him. Tell us, and the pain will stop.'

The soldiers told more and more lies. Some said they had killed the Czar with their pikes, others with their swords. Some said they had strangled him with rope. Some said they had buried the parts of the Czar in the yard, others that they had thrown them into the river, others that they had thrown them on to a rubbish heap behind the kitchens. Some of them could stand the torture no longer and died.

The yard was dug up, the rubbish heap searched, and no body of the Czar was found. Back the torturers came. 'Why didn't you tell us the truth? Now we have to begin again until you tell us the truth.' And the torture went on until all the soldiers who had been with the Czar were dead. The truth was still not known. Torture is not for discovering the truth: it is for the pleasure of the torturers.

Did the soldiers' fear, under torture, ever become as great as that of those they had tortured and murdered at the Czar's pleasure? Let us, says the cat, feel sorry for the tortured soldiers, but let us not forget that they were torturers too.

What became of the Czardom? asks the cat. A

nephew of the Czar was declared the new Czar by some of the nobles, but others wished to see one of the Czar's cousins made Czar instead. There was a short war, and the nephew won, because he had most of the nobles on his side, which meant he had most of the money, most of the soldiers, most of the cannon.

But even after the war was won, and the new Czar safe on his throne, the Czar Grozni was not forgotten. His most sacred person had been murdered by evil-doers – that was what the new Czar said. The Czar Grozni had been God on Earth, a most holy and devout man, so beloved of God that God had sent him an angel. But mankind was so wicked that this martyr, this saint, had been murdered by the guard he loved and trusted. A church was built to him, and the walls painted with scenes from his life. The biggest picture was of the coming of the Black Angel.

At the centre of the church was a gilded and jewelled shrine, where the Czar's body was believed to be buried, and there people came to pray for for-giveness of their sins – and not one of them who prayed there had committed as many sins as the Czar Grozni.

But even the church and the shrine could not quite silence another story: that the Czar Grozni had been so cruel and so wicked that his true master, the Devil, had come up from Hell and carried him away. It was hard to say how this story spread, because no one dared to tell it. 'May you warm your feet where Czar Grozni warms his feet,' people would say. 'In the next life, may you find yourself beside Czar Grozni.' And if you believed that this was a wish for you to go to Heaven, no one would put you right.

People were afraid to tell the story about Grozni and the Devil because Grozni's nephew was the new Czar, and he wouldn't like it – but there was another reason, another story. This said that Czar Grozni was not dead, but alive and hiding, playing a trick on his people, to see how they would behave in his absence. He was going about the land in disguise, said the story. Any stranger might really be the Czar Grozni. Treat him well, and you would be rewarded in time; treat him badly, and his revenge would be terrible. Even a hundred and fifty years after Grozni's death, this story was believed. After all, Grozni had been so favoured of God that God had sent him an angel: he had been a Czar and a saint. Anything was possible for a Czar and a saint, even to live two hundred years.

But what (asks the cat) of Shingebiss?

Her spirit did not follow the soldiers from the work-room, out into the cold yard, where the wind would have blown her into threads. Instead she hung in the candlelight beside Christian's body, and she went spirit-travelling again. She knew that he had never learned anything of the Ghost World, and would not find his way there. She went looking for him in the places where the lost and unguided spirits go . . .

Which was into those formless places between worlds, between dreams. Long, dark, endless walk-ings into nothing. Endless mutterings of voices, of unseen people, saying nothing. Nothing for the feet to touch, and nothing to be seen – the shapelessness, the chaos that lies behind all worlds.

So many, many people lost here; so many that had lost all form and no longer remembered who or what they had been. So many nameless, unrecognizable, unrescuable. Shingebiss passed them by in silence, and they didn't know she was among them.

A voice was calling in the darkness, calling on a ragged note of panic and distress. 'Christian!' it cried out, and again and again. 'Christian!'

Shingebiss followed that voice. She came upon Master Jenkins's wandering and frightened spirit, and she buffeted him like a strong wind. She hissed in his ear, and he cringed and remembered stories of Hell and demons poking lost souls with pitchforks into pits of fire. And then, leaving him, she passed on, and found Christian.

Just as, when we dream, we have a dream-body, so a spirit has a body. And Shingebiss stepped close to Christian in the darkness and put her hand into his.

He started with surprise and pulled away from her. Christian didn't know that he was dead, nor where he was, nor what were the murmurings and mutterings he heard all about him. 'What? What?' he cried out; and at his outcry, there were more cries of shock and fear from the darkness all around.

Shingebiss said, 'I am the Black Angel.'

'The Angel? The Czar's Black Angel? Will you – Angel, please – will you take me back to my master?'

'No.'

She felt Christian's hand twist in hers. 'Then why have you come?'

'To take you home.'

Christian's whisper came through the darkness. 'Denmark?'

As he spoke, the darkness was growing lighter around him. He closed his eyes, fearing to see the faces belonging to those frightened, muttering voices he had heard all around him; but through half-closed eyes he saw the shapes of trees. He opened his eyes and saw that he stood in a forest of fir and birch. He smelt the earth and the resin. A squirrel ran up a tree above his head and showered bark-dust down on him. And in front of him, holding his hand, stood the Black Angel, its black, black hair falling in nets and tangles around its shoulders.

'Is this Denmark?'

'No,' said the Black Angel, and it turned away from him and led him, by the hand, through the forest. Christian looked about him, at the black earth, and the deep beds of pine needles that made their walking silent. He looked up at the blue sky between the tops of the dark pines. He reached out and touched the trunk of a tree. It was a real forest.

'Where was I before? I think I heard my Master calling – '

'You were lost,' said the Angel.

Christian remembered a long dark room, where his Master had also been – and the Czar – and soldiers. He couldn't tell if it was a real memory.

The Black Angel led him to a village built in the forest. There were little storerooms standing on poles, and pens holding reindeer. Men and women were sitting outside one of the houses, listening to the telling of a story. The story ended at the sight of Shingebiss and Christian. The people were Northlanders, and they knew a shaman when they saw one. Respectfully, they all stood.

'This is Christian,' Shingebiss said. 'I leave him to your care.' And to Christian she said, 'If you don't like it here, walk that way. Cross the stream and you will come to Iron Wood.'

And then, refusing all offers of food and drink, the shaman went away. As far as I know (says the cat), Christian stayed in the village – for eternity. This village was built in the Ghost World. Though the forest around it seemed to pass through seasons, though there seemed to be night and day, in truth, no time passed. When a tree was felled, it stood again the next day. When a reindeer was killed, if the bones were kept whole and wrapped in a portion of its skin, the reindeer lived again the morning after. No one grew older and no one died.

Some grew bored. When that happened, they went into the forest, and crossed the stream and walked into Iron Wood. And, occasionally, some sleepwalker from Iron Wood wandered across the stream into their forest and was brought by the people of the village to live with them.

And Shingebiss (asks the cat)?

A gyrfalcon rose into the twilight of the Ghost World, rising and turning among the branches of the trees, and flew high over the Ghost World Gate and back into this world.

Flying far, flying high, the gyrfalcon looked down on the dish of the world. It saw long black strings leaving the few cities and straggling out into the Northlands – armies of men. Sweeping over their heads, the gyrfalcon looked down and saw them fell trees to build townships to shelter them while they cut more trees. The falcon saw the rivers choked with rafts of tree-trunks, saw the forests vanish, saw the wind and rain wash away the soil that the trees had held in place. What had once grown there would never grow again. *Keeee-ya!*

The gyrfalcon swooped down and lighted on the gibbets outside the hunters' camps. There, freezing in the freezing wind, hung wolf skins, and reindeer skins, skins of puma, bear and fox. The gyrfalcon took to the air again and, looking down, saw the animals leaving, starving, dying as their land was taken from them.

The gyrfalcon, flying, flying, watching, watching, saw the reindeer people being driven through the stumps of their forest, roped one behind another; driven south to be sold as slaves. The new Czar had no objections to trading with the West.

The gyrfalcon turned in the air and looked down and saw the reindeer people being slaughtered, by families, by tribes, to clear the land.

The gyrfalcon looked down and watched the Northlands come to that desolation Hel desired. And even the tree-fellers in their townships, and the hunters in their camps, even they heard the wind asking, as it passed, 'Are you cold, my children? Are you cold?'

The gyrfalcon turned and watched the cities grow

where the forests had been, but where no ghost songs had been sung for all that had been slaughtered there. The gyrfalcon lighted on church porches, on house-roofs, on palace towers, and watched the people of the cities grow peevish, and frightened and sick, watched them tear at each other, and live long lives, but die without knowing the way to the Ghost World.

And then the gyrfalcon spread its wings and flew back over the Gate into the Ghost World, where Balder dreamed and Hel listened to her music; into Iron Wood, where the Czar Grozni lay, dreaming more pain and torture into this world.

In the Ghost World, beyond Iron Wood, lay all that was left of the Northlands; and in that timeless Northlands forest there is a gyrfalcon. It has been a gyrfalcon so long, it has almost forgotten that it was once a mortal baby, and then a shaman's apprentice and a shaman, and a Czar's black angel.

And that is the end of this story (says the cat).

If you thought it tasty, then serve it to others.

If you thought it sour, sweeten it with your own telling.

But whether you liked it, or liked it not, let it make its own way back to me, riding on another's tongue.

The cat lays herself down among the links of her golden chain and tucks her forepaws beneath her breast. Head up, ears pricked, she falls asleep under her oak tree, and neither sings nor tells stories.